M000191762

CHAPTER 1

KAREN GLICK FINISHED TYING her apron strings around her
back as she hurried to get to her Saturday job at the Amish
bishop's household. Their house was a little less than a mile
away from Karen's home; not far enough to hitch and
unhitch the buggy except in the wintertime. She helped out
every Saturday, and Hannah, the bishop's wife, needed her
more than ever seeing she was soon to give birth to their
thirteenth child.

The children were all boys except for the second oldest,
Rebecca, who was fourteen. Karen had a sneaking suspicion
the bishop and his wife were hoping for another girl; they'd
never say so.

Saturday, weather permitting, was nominated the second
laundry-day of the week for the Shroder household. It was
unbelievable how the children could get through so much
clothing, but everything was multiplied by twelve and then
there were the two adults.

As Karen approached the house, she saw the children
kicking a ball around in one of the paddocks. That was
unusual for so early in the morning. In the summer months,

1

the children often played in the fields in the afternoon after they had finished their chores.

There was a horse and buggy parked outside the house, which wasn't unusual. The bishop had many daily visitors and greeted them in the front room of the house where it was quiet, away from the children.

She'd given up knocking a long time ago. Nowadays she walked in because she was rarely ever heard if she knocked, especially at the back door.

∼

As Jason listened to the bishop, his uncle on his father's side, he looked out the window and saw a slender young woman walking briskly toward the house. He couldn't help but admire the look of determination on her attractive face, but why that faraway look in her eyes? He knew that look. This young woman carried a burden just as he did.

The bishop stopped talking and followed his gaze. "That's our Karen. She helps Hannah on Saturdays."

"Our Karen?"

Bishop Elmer Shroder chuckled and stroked his silver beard. "She's like our adopted *dochder,* and it's no secret that she was adopted and her adoptive parents are now with *Gott.* Hannah and I are very fond of her. She helps out here at the *haus* every Saturday. If we'd had more girls we'd have no need of outside help. The boys do their fair share, though. They don't escape household chores because of the lack of women. The work has to get done and it can't all fall onto Rebecca and Hannah."

"Married?" he asked of the young woman he'd seen.

The bishop looked over the top of his thin-rimmed round glasses. *"Nee,* she's not." He pointed his finger at Jason. "And

2

THE AMISH WOMAN AND HER LAST HOPE

AMISH WOMEN OF PLEASANT VALLEY

SAMANTHA PRICE

AMISH ROMANCE

Copyright © 2018 by Samantha Price

All rights reserved.

No part of this book may be reproduced in any form or by any electronic or mechanical means, including information storage and retrieval systems, without written permission from the author, except for the use of brief quotations in a book review.

This book is a work of fiction. Any resemblance to any person, living or dead, is purely coincidental. The personal names have been invented by the author, and any likeness to the name of any person, living or dead, is purely coincidental.

Scripture quotations from The Authorized (King James) Version. Rights in the Authorized Version in the United Kingdom are vested in the Crown. Reproduced by permission of the Crown's patentee, Cambridge University Press.

Print ISBN 978-1-925689-60-0

come to think of it, she just might suit you. Hannah tries to find her a husband all the time."

That made her sound less attractive, as though she'd been passed over many a time. "Why has she never married? Is there something wrong with her?"

The bishop was silent for a while, appearing taken aback by the brutal question. "I can ask the same of you."

Jason shrugged his shoulders realizing the bishop was right. He, too, was single, and could be looked upon in the same unflattering light. "There's been no one suitable for me … apparently." He had thought he'd found someone until the relationship had come crashing down around him like an old barn during a storm. There was a woman for him out there waiting somewhere—there had to be.

"Don't you think it's the same for her?"

"What was that?" Jason had been lost in his own thoughts.

"You've found no one you like enough to marry; don't you think it's the same for her?"

"Maybe. Unless there's something you're not telling me?" He stared at the bishop to see if he was holding anything back. What if he was, because he was fonder of Karen than he was his own nephew? When the bishop offered no further information, Jason had to probe further. "Does she have any vices?"

The bishop laughed. "We're not talking about a horse here. As far as I know she doesn't kick or bite."

Jason smiled and then looked out the window hoping to catch another glimpse, but the woman had gone around the corner. "She seems upset about something."

"There's nothing wrong with her. She's had a few worries. I can assure you, you couldn't do better than to find a woman such as Karen."

"That's good enough for me." Maybe there was hope for him after all.

The bishop leaned forward. "Perhaps we can invite you to dinner on Monday night?"

"You mean Karen will be at dinner too?"

A big smile broke out on the bishop's face. "We'll invite her and see how you both get along."

He hadn't intended to find a woman while he was here. His sole intention in coming to Pleasant Valley was to sort himself out, and figure out what to do with the bakery. "*Denke.* I'd like that very much."

"How long can you stay?"

"I'm only intending to be here for a week."

"That's not long if you're trying to find a *fraa.*"

Jason laughed. "*Onkel* Elmer, I told you I was here looking for work ideas." That was kind of true.

"Your *vadder* told me the bakery's doing well. How come you'd want to change your vocation?"

He didn't want to bore his uncle with the whole sorry tale. "I'm exploring my options."

Uncle Elmer stared at him blankly. It was a look Jason had seen on his father's face many a time. In their day, they were raised working hard in the fields and didn't have a choice. The older generation never understood how the younger men of today wanted to find different ways of making money and find job satisfaction along the way.

Jason smiled and added, "If things go well, I might be able to stretch my stay a little longer." He then stood. "I should go. *Denke, Onkel,* for the loan of the buggy for the week. Do you want anything while I'm in town?"

"I don't, but you could ask Hannah. Women are always needing something from the store. Or, they always think they do."

"I'll do that."

~

KAREN FOUND Hannah in the kitchen washing a pile of dishes stacked halfway to the ceiling. "Morning, Hannah. Do you want me to finish up in here?"

Hannah turned around, her pregnant tummy just missing the kitchen cabinets. *"Nee,* I'll finish these. Good morning to you. Do you mind filling and starting the washing machine?"

"Sure. I mean, I don't mind, and I'll get started on it. You have a visitor?"

She looked at Karen, a peculiar smile on her face. "A young man from out of town."

"Oh?"

"When you get the first load going, I might take you to meet him."

"Okay." Hannah was always interested in meeting the men who passed through their community. In the past, she'd had crushes on men, but nothing had ever worked out. There was certainly no one in her own community who suited her. There were plenty of young men but, already being twenty-eight, the single men were way too young for her. The couples usually paired up before they were twenty, leaving Karen with little prospect of a suitable match. Karen had already half-resigned herself to the fact she'd never marry but, she figured, there was always hope.

∼

AFTER JASON FINISHED TALKING to his *Onkel* Elmer, he headed to the kitchen to find Hannah. She was nowhere about, but he heard sounds in the adjacent room. "Hannah?" He stuck his head around the door. It was the young woman he'd seen earlier, and he'd startled her. "Oh, I'm sorry." She'd been placing clothes into the gas-powered washing machine.

She straightened up and smoothed down her dress, barely looking him in the eye. She was prettier up close and although she wasn't a raving beauty something attracted him to her. She was just the right height to rest his arm comfortably around her shoulders.

"You gave me quite a fright," she finally said, making him realize he'd been standing there staring at her for a little too long.

"I'm sorry," he repeated. He stretched out his hand. "I'm Jason Shroder."

CHAPTER 2

KAREN SHOOK HIS HAND, noticing how strong it was. She quickly pulled her hand back and placed it by her side, and stood there feeling awkward under the gaze of his incredible blue eyes. "Hello, Jason. I'm Karen Glick."

"I'm staying here with my *onkel* and aunt for a few days. The bishop is also my *onkel,* but I'm staying with *Onkel* Peter next door. *Onkel* Elmer said you help out here every Saturday."

The man was talking at a million miles per minute, but he was around her age and she was interested to know more. "That's right. I have done so for quite a while."

HE LIKED the way she spoke. She had a gleam of intelligence in her eyes, and he guessed she was a woman who knew what she wanted. There was a moment between them and he was sure she knew, too, there was an attraction. "Do you live close by?"

She smiled and nodded. "Within walking distance."

"Can I offer you a ride home?"

She giggled putting her fingertips to her lips. "I only just got here."

"On your way home, I meant. Whenever you're ready. Later today?"

She nodded. "I'd like that, *denke*. Where are you staying? You're not staying here?"

"*Nee*, on the next farm. With Peter and Barbara."

She was trying to make conversation, but then remembered he'd told her that already. "*Jah*, sorry, you just told me that. My brain is still a bit rattled from being startled."

"While I'm here I'm using one of Elmer's buggies. He has a spare, and Peter doesn't. Anyway, I have to go into town now and I was just coming to find Hannah to ask if she needed anything."

"I think she's upstairs checking on the *boppli*." Joel, the baby was eighteen months old but was still called 'the *boppli'* by everyone and probably would be until the next addition to the family arrived.

"I'll find her." He looked down at the washing machine. "You're doing a good job there."

"You know about washing?"

He stood straight. "You know, that's a good question. I don't know a thing about washing."

"Does your *mudder* wash your clothes?"

He didn't like that question. The answer would make him seem too young and not at all independent. He could see by the glimmer of a smile on her lips she was teasing him. "Mostly ... I'm embarrassed to admit. She doesn't have one of these new ones. She has one of the ones with the double sink. I think that's what you call them." She laughed and he wasn't sure if she was laughing at him or with him. "I guess it's time I learned to do things like that for myself."

"Maybe." She turned away and started filling the machine again. Then she stopped and looked up at him. "You don't have a *fraa?*"

"I'm working on it." He could've kicked himself for saying that. "I mean, I don't have anyone, and I'm working on that at the moment. And yourself?"

She shook her head. "I have no *fraa.*"

He laughed when he saw her grinning. She was quite funny. "And no husband either, I hope?"

"Nee. If I did, I might be doing all this at my own home."

"Good point. I should've figured that one out for myself."

She glanced up at him and gave him a bright smile before she looked back at the washing.

"So, what time would you allow me to drive you home?" he asked.

"I finish at four. Will you be back by then?"

"I'll be back well before then. I'll make sure of it. I'll go look for Hannah."

"Bye, Jason."

Tingles ran through his body at the way she said his name. Despite the fright he'd caused her, she'd taken care to remember it. He'd never felt this way about any woman at first meeting. He'd only been in love once and that had developed over time.

$\sim$

KAREN IMMEDIATELY LIKED the young man who'd startled her in the laundry room. He seemed a little younger than the ideal man she'd envisioned, but it would be a difficult and almost impossible thing to find a suitable and still-single man her age. Knowing Hannah and Jason would be talking upstairs, once she turned on the washing machine, she busied herself cleaning the kitchen countertops. She'd stay here until Hannah came down and told her what to do next. It was different every week.

As she was wiping down the sink, she noticed Jason walking out to the buggy. He climbed in, took up the reins in his strong tanned hands, and then glanced in the direction of the kitchen. She looked away immediately, not wanting him to know she'd been watching. He wasn't an overly handsome man, but he did have a pleasant face and he was tall, which was a bonus.

"It seems you met Jason, our nephew."

Karen swung around to see Hannah. *"Ach, jah.* We had a little talk."

"He told me all about it. Are you able to come for the evening meal on Monday night?"

Had Jason been talking about her? "I'd love to. Will Jason still be here? I mean here for dinner, on Monday night?"

"Jah. If you'll be here he'll definitely be here for the evening meal.*"

"Then I'll definitely be here too."

Hannah tipped her head to one side and grinned. "Like that, is it?"

"It might be." She giggled and thought she should focus on the reason she was there. "What are we doing today?"

"We've got to give the *boppli's* room a good clean."

"You're making a separate room for the new one?"

Hannah laughed. *"Nee,* we don't have room to spare enough for that and it wouldn't be fair on the others. The new *boppli* will have to stay in with Elmer and me. I'm talking about the room where we've got the four youngest."

Karen took hold of the bucket of cleaning items and Hannah picked up a fistful of rags and they headed up the stairs.

"How are you doing with those extensions you were talking about for the *haus?*" Karen asked as they moved a bed so they could clean underneath.

"It's something we'll get around to eventually, but we keep putting it off because we keep adding to the *familye.*"

"I know it would be a strain to live around the building work, even though the result would be such a blessing."

"I think we'd all have to move out and that's way too much for me to think about right now. Ideally, I'd like Rebecca to have a room of her own now that she's getting older."

"Who does she share with now?" Karen asked.

"Peter, Charles, and Aedan."

Karen knew those were the young school age ones, around the ages of six through eight. "I'd definitely say she needs a room of her own at this age. I imagine it's not easy being the only girl. She needs a place to get away from them all."

"She never complains."

"She could always come and live with me. I have a spare room."

Hannah laughed. "Maybe when she's older, but by then you might have a *familye* of your own."

"I hope so. It would be nice."

"Speaking of you getting married, Jason tells me he's driving you home this afternoon."

She looked up and saw the sparkle in Hannah's eyes. *"Jah.* Don't get too excited. It doesn't mean we'll get married. I told him I live close, but a ride home would save my feet after a long day's work."

"I don't work you that hard, do I?"

Karen laughed. *"Nee,* but I couldn't refuse him. Not when he looked at me with those big blue eyes."

Hannah laughed. "Eyes, that's what first attracted me to Elmer."

Karen tried to picture Elmer as a young man but couldn't.

CHAPTER 3

THE CHORES WENT much quicker that day for Karen because all she could think about was Jason. A man could have no better recommendation than being the nephew of the bishop and nephew of Peter, the bishop's brother. From what she'd gleaned so far, Jason was polite and handsome, and came from a good family. What more could she want in a man? She couldn't wait to find out more about him on the drive home. It seemed all her prayers were finally being answered. She liked his sense of fun, offering to drive her the short distance that she could've easily walked. The ride would only take five or ten minutes at most.

She would need to find out what kind of work he did and if he was tied to his own community with a job or strong family ties. Ideally, after she married she'd like to stay put in Pleasant Valley. She didn't want to move away and have to get used to a different place with people she didn't know. If they married, would he move here with her, or would she be expected to leave her home and move to live with him?

Of course, it was far too early to be worried about these

things, but she was a planner and had been that way all of her life. If she didn't have a plan or at least an idea where she was headed in life, she was anxious. It was the circumstances of her birth and the adoption that caused her to feel the need for a sense of control. She'd figured out that was what it was, and whomever she married would have to be comfortable with her being like that.

As SHE BUSIED herself pinning out the clean clothes to dry, Rebecca came out of the house.

"What do you think of my cousin?" Rebecca leaned down and picked up a shirt from the basket.

"Jason?"

"*Jah*, Jason."

"He seems nice. He's giving me a ride home."

Rebecca giggled. "He is? You're going on a date already? He moved quickly."

"It's not a date. It's just a buggy ride and I get tired after doing chores here all day."

Rebecca grinned and pinned the shirt to the line. "I can't believe you've never met him. He's been here two or three times in the last few years."

"Has he? I wonder why I don't remember him."

"I don't know." Rebecca shook her head and placed her hands on her hips. "Maybe you thought he was unremarkable."

Karen gave a little giggle. "Come on, are you helping me or what?" Karen thought Jason *was* remarkable now, even if she hadn't noticed him on other visits. And, she hoped she'd find him even more remarkable later in the day. For Karen, there was nothing like the excitement of liking someone and feeling the nervousness of a stomach full of butterflies.

Unfortunately, the handful of men she'd been 'in like with' in her younger years hadn't reciprocated with similar feelings. She'd admired them from afar, never letting them know how she felt. That way she was safe from the bitter pangs of rejection.

Rebecca pinned out more laundry. "I think my cousin might be just the man for you."

"Do you now?"

"He's grown quite handsome and he's kind. He was always kind to me. I remember one day when we were younger and my *bruder* had saved up his pocket money and wanted something in town. My parents said no, they wouldn't take us to town, and then he said yes. And he took those of us who were old enough all the way into town to the store. That's always stuck in my head."

"What did your *bruder* want?"

"It was a useless new knife. Probably for his whittling."

"It might be useless to you or me, but I'm sure it wasn't useless to your *bruder*."

"I suppose not. But it's things like that that you remember about people. A small act of kindness says a lot about a person."

Karen smiled at Rebecca's enthusiasm, but didn't want to get her hopes up and fall in love with Jason before she knew him. The only thing she could do was put him out of her mind for the rest of the day.

BY MID-AFTERNOON, Karen was finishing off the dusting in the living room when Rebecca hurried into the room like a whirlwind. *"Mamm* said you can call it good for today."

"Really?"

"Jah."

"Okay." Karen looked at the china clock she had just dusted. She wasn't due to finish for fifteen more minutes.

Rebecca said, "Why don't I make you a cup of *kaffe?*"

Karen was pleasantly shocked. It was the first time Rebecca had ever made such an offer. "I've had one today already, thanks. I normally only have one in the morning before I begin the day."

"Oh, come on. Have one with me. It won't kill you."

Karen giggled. "Okay, just a small one."

"Let's go." Rebecca grabbed the dusting rag and hurried away. "C'mon."

"Hey! I need that duster."

"*Mamm* said you're finished now," Rebecca called over her shoulder with a grin.

Karen hurried after her, giggling, and grabbed the dusting rag from the clean kitchen table where Rebecca had tossed it. "Hey, girl, I just polished this table."

"It's still clean."

Karen shook her head, still smiling at Rebecca's silliness, and threw the rag into the bag in the laundry room and washed her hands.

"Where are you going?" Rebecca asked.

Karen stepped back into the room. "Just finishing up. Okay, now I'm ready for *kaffe.*" She sat down at the table. "Where's your *mudder?*"

"She's upstairs making the beds."

"Doesn't everyone make their own beds?" Karen knew they did.

"We do, but the little ones didn't make them properly today, so *Mamm's* showing them how to do it—again."

"Ah, I see."

"*Mamm's* so particular about everything."

"I don't blame her. With so many *kinner* she'd have to be

pretty particular, otherwise there'd be nothing but calamity and chaos."

Rebecca pulled some mugs out of the cupboard. "I thought it would be the opposite way. If I ever have so many children I would be happy if things got done at all. I wouldn't drive myself mad worrying about every little detail."

"You might change your mind when you get older."

"I don't think so." While the hot water boiled, Rebecca sat down. "I wonder when my cousin will return."

Just then they heard a buggy and Rebecca jumped up and looked out the window. "Here he is now. In time to have a cup of coffee with us. How convenient."

"That would be nice," Karen said, hoping Rebecca wouldn't say something embarrassing. Or, maybe Rebecca would leave the two of them alone to have coffee together. She was just about to give Rebecca a hint to do so when Hannah walked into the kitchen ruining her plan before it began.

"That's Jason just arrived back. Isn't he giving you a ride home?" Hannah absently rubbed her belly in a light circular motion as she spoke, and Karen wondered just how uncomfortable it was to be that far pregnant.

"That's right," Karen answered.

"I'm just making Karen some *kaffe*," Rebecca told her mother. "Do you want a hot tea, *Mamm?*"

"I wouldn't mind one. And find some of those peanut cookies we made yesterday, *jah?*"

They heard the front door open. "We're in the kitchen, Jason," Rebecca called out.

"Rebecca, what have I told you about screaming?" Hannah glared at her daughter.

"It wasn't a scream."

"It was raising your voice and that is not allowed in this *haus.*"

"Sorry, *Mamm.*" She then muttered under her breath, "I don't know how he was supposed to hear where we were if I didn't yell."

Hannah sat down at the table, and either didn't hear that comment, or chose to ignore it.

CHAPTER 4

JASON WALKED into the kitchen with Timothy, Rebecca's oldest *bruder.*

"Jason, you have to have *kaffe* with us before you set out on the long journey to take Karen home," Rebecca said, as she jumped up to turn off the kettle that had just started to whistle.

Jason looked at Karen. "Do we have time, Karen?"

"I do, if you do."

He smiled. *"Kaffe,* would be nice *denke."*

"I'll have a hot tea please, Rebecca," Timothy said.

As soon as Timothy and Jason sat down, Jason asked, "Do you work, Karen, besides here on Saturdays?"

"I do. I work at the lumberyard."

Rebecca butted in, "She works at the lumberyard that Samuel Kauffman owns. And she lives in a *haus* he owns too."

Jason said, "Samuel owns half of Pleasant Valley it seems. I know the lumberyard he owns. It's out on Willow Creek Road just past the old mill."

"That's right," Karen said.

"I was planning on going there tomorrow. That's a coincidence."

When Rebecca burst into giggles, Jason's face twisted into a smile. "I was, my jolly young cousin. I was going there tomorrow."

"Tomorrow is Sunday," Timothy told him.

Jason laughed. "So it is, so it is. I meant Monday. Of course, I wouldn't go on a Sunday. I meant the very next working day, which is Monday."

"Why would you buy timber here when you live so far away?" Rebecca asked.

"Because, Rebecca, there's such a thing as transport. We don't build houses anymore with the trees we chopped down ourselves. Haven't you learned that?"

"Forgive them, Jason, they've forgotten their manners lately," Hannah said. "You'll both be back at the children's table for dinner tonight if you don't stop your nonsense," Hannah told them.

Rebecca held her stomach and laughed hard at what her mother said, while Timothy's face fell. Karen felt a little sorry for Timothy at being grouped together with Rebecca like that. All he'd done was point out that the next day was Sunday.

Hannah moved her seat back slightly. "Go to your room now, Rebecca."

"I didn't yell, *Mamm,* I was just laughing."

"You're being too noisy for a young lady. Go up to your room and stay there until you think about what you've done."

Rebecca pouted. "I just thought about what I've done, and I'm sorry."

Hannah's face went hard like a rock and her lips pressed together tightly, and then she said, "I think what you've done here deserves half an hour in your room."

Rebecca placed her hands on her hips. "Who's gonna make the *kaffe?*"

"I can make it," Karen said.

Hannah shook her head. "I'll make it, and you can have an hour in your room, Rebecca."

Rebecca stomped out of the room.

"I feel so sorry for her," Karen said before she could stop herself.

"Nothing to be sorry about," Hannah said. "Give them an inch and they'll take a mile. She's been obstinate lately."

"She has a vibrant personality," Jason said.

"If by vibrant you mean loud, then I will agree with you," Hannah said.

Karen nodded, and added, "Perhaps she feels she has to be noisy to be heard over the boys."

"You mean me?" Timothy put his hands up. "I'm tryin' to stay out of it."

"Nee, not you, the younger ones," Karen said.

"How have you been, Hannah?" Jason asked as she got up to set about making the coffees and the teas.

"I've been very well this time around."

"And you are hoping for another boy?" he asked.

"Elmer and I will be pleased with whatever *Gott* blesses us with. We don't mind one way or the other." She placed three cups of hot tea down on the table and then sat down, even though two of them were expecting coffee.

"Aren't you having one?" Jason asked Hannah.

"Nee, I'll leave you young people to talk. I'll check on how the little ones are getting on with making their beds." She stood and hurried out of the room.

"It must be hard for her walking up and down stairs all day long," Karen said.

Jason smiled and nodded and then sipped his tea. "Ah, that's good coffee."

Karen giggled. He'd made no comment about getting tea rather than coffee. A very good decision under the circumstances.

Timothy stood. "I just remembered I've got something to do. Excuse me."

"Certainly," Jason said.

Karen poured a little milk into her tea, and then heaped two teaspoons of sugar into it and then tasted it. By then Timothy was out of the room. "Mmm, it is good."

"And what do you do at the lumberyard?"

"I look after the ordering and the invoicing."

"So, you're good at math?"

Karen shrugged. She was just average at everything and had no special skills. "Adequate, I'd say. I haven't had any complaints."

"I guess that's a good thing."

"And do you have any sisters or brothers, Jason?"

"I have three younger brothers."

"How much younger?"

"There's quite a gap between me and my brothers. There are the twins who are fifteen and the other brother is eighteen."

She smiled at him and was lost for words. She wouldn't mind having twins and she was pleased they ran in his family. She pushed the plate of cookies towards him. "Want a cookie?"

"*Denke.*" He kept smiling at her and didn't take his eyes from her even when he reached for a cookie.

Then they heard someone walk in the back door. They both turned to see Bishop Elmer walk into the kitchen, destroying their brief time alone. "Ah, there you are." Bishop Elmer looked at Karen. "Were you able to come for dinner Monday night?"

"I am coming. *Denke* for asking. I'm looking forward to it."

Unaware that Timothy and Hannah had strategically left them alone, the bishop sat down at the table with them.

"Would you like a hot drink?" Karen asked him.

"Jah, denke."

The younger boys came inside and politely excused themselves for butting into the adults' conversation. Then they asked Jason to play ball with them. Karen was pleased when he told them he would when he got back from driving Karen home. That showed he was kind, just as Rebecca had told her. The boys smiled and hurried back outside.

"They have such lovely manners," Karen said.

Hannah came back into the room just in time to hear Karen's words. "Let's hope they don't forget them when they get older like a certain person."

"I hope you're not talking about me," Jason said with a smile.

"Nee, I think you can guess who I'm talking about."

Bishop Elmer sighed. "What's she done now?"

"Nothing too much. I'm not letting her get away with anything lately."

"Good," the bishop said.

Hannah sat down with them. On hearing the children playing outdoors, Karen said to Jason, "Why don't you have a quick game with them now before you take me home?"

"You don't mind?"

"Nee. I'm not in a hurry."

"Okay." He excused himself, then took his mug to the sink and poured out the contents. "Come find me when you're ready, Karen."

"I will."

Once he was gone, Hannah said to Elmer, "I think Karen thinks I'm too harsh on Rebecca."

"*Nee,* I don't, not exactly that. I just feel a little sympathy for her being the only girl with so many brothers, and not having any private space at this age. I mean, I guess you have to be strict."

The bishop adjusted his glasses and looked over at Karen. "The girl needs to know discipline if she's ever to raise her own *kinner.*"

"A lot falls onto her shoulders and always has and that means we must be stricter," Hannah further explained.

Karen nodded. "I believe you. It must be hard to know just how strict to be."

The bishop said, "You can always let their behavior be your guide. Like a horse going the wrong way changes direction with a small wrist movement that in turn moves the reins."

"You'll know when you get to that stage of parenting," Hannah said. "What you need to concentrate on now is finding yourself a man."

Karen looked down at her tea and out of the corner of her eye noticed the bishop and his wife exchanging glances. She was certain they had Jason on their minds. It was an awkward moment.

CHAPTER 5

KAREN SAID goodbye to Hannah and the bishop, and then walked out the door to find Jason. She followed the laughter around to the back of the house. For Karen, there was no sound more pleasing than children enjoying themselves.

Jason looked over and saw her, and hurried toward her followed by three of the younger boys. "Are you ready?" he asked.

"Where are you going, Karen? Can we come?" one of the boys called out.

They looked at her, and then she said, "You'll have to ask your cousin."

"Denke," he said quietly out of the side of his mouth causing her to giggle. He looked down at the boys. "You can't come today, but I'll take you somewhere another day. Okay?"

"We haven't finished our ball game," one of them groaned.

"I'll play with you some more tomorrow. We'll take up where we left off."

One boy grabbed a brother and whispered in his ear and then they both giggled and ran off, trailed by the third brother.

"I don't know what that was all about," Jason said as he looked back at Karen.

"*Nee*, neither do I." She had a pretty good idea, though. At that age, most children found the idea of boyfriends and girl-friends particularly funny.

"Are you ready?" Jason asked again.

"I am."

THEY STEPPED up into the buggy and he took up the reins. When he turned the horse to face the road, the horse started down the driveway. Looking over at Karen, he asked, "Which way?"

"When you get out onto the road you go left and then take the first right and then I'm just over the bridge, first house on the right."

"Got it." When he got down to the road, he directed the horse to the right.

"I said to go left."

"Are you sure?"

She laughed. "I think I know the way to my own *haus*."

"I thought you said right."

"I said first go left and then right, and then it's the first place on the right over the bridge."

"Oh, okay. I have trouble concentrating with you in the buggy with me." He glanced over at her and gave her a big grin and she couldn't keep the smile from her face.

"Am I making you nervous?" she asked.

"You must be, if you're making me forget which is my left and right. It's difficult for me, you see. The teacher always used to say, 'You write with your right hand,' but I'm left handed so I have been mixed up ever since. I was the only left-handed one in the class. She tried to make me right handed, but then gave up on that idea when my parents objected. They believed it was God who made me this way and that was that."

She smiled at him. "So, it's not me making you nervous? You seriously don't know your left from your right?"

He chuckled. "I'm only joking about that. I do know my left from my right. And, you are making me nervous."

"Good to know." Then she remembered her list of questions. "Are you on holiday from your job?"

"I'm kind of between jobs at the moment."

She hoped he wasn't a drifter. She'd seen a few of them passing through the community. They had no direction in life and were going from place to place looking for a wife to take back home with them. But, home to what? A lifetime of struggle and uncertainty? She didn't mind working hard, but she wanted a man who worked just as hard or more so. Her friend's husband didn't work much and she was sure it led to all kinds of problems in their marriage and with his state of mind. "What do you normally do when you're working?"

"I do a bit of this and a bit of that. Some roofing and building work, but I'm trying to get out of that into a different line of work. I had a nasty fall and injured my back. I'm okay now, but I figure that kind of work … Well, I don't think my body would last long if I did that sort of work day after day for years."

"Is that why you're here? Are you looking for a job?"

"*Jah.* I came to talk things over with my two *onkels.* I've got a few ideas up my sleeve, and I wanted to run some options by them."

"That's a good idea. It always pays to get advice from your elders." She glanced at him when he looked in his rearview mirror. The afternoon sun hit his face and highlighted his strong and angular features. She'd be very happy to wake up and look at that face every day of her life. Then he moved and the sun streamed into her eyes. She raised her hand to shield them from the sun.

He glanced over at her. "Sun's in your eyes?"

"Just a little."

"It'll change when we turn the corner."

She noticed his clothes were nicely sewn and knew his mother had most likely made them. That reminded her to finish the half-made dress she had at home. She'd have to do it tonight; their community didn't allow sewing on a Sunday as it was considered to be work. Tomorrow her friends, Mary and Beth, were visiting. Visiting was what folks in their community did on the second Sunday where there was no church service.

"First *haus* after the bridge, so this must be it."

"This is the one." She pointed to the barn. "I share that barn with the neighbors. Mary and Damian. Mary is a good friend of mine, which is convenient seeing that we share the barn."

"I'm guessing that Samuel owns both places?"

"That's right."

He pulled up the buggy. "It looks like a nice *haus*."

"It's quite small, but it suits me. I thank *Gott* nearly every day for blessing me with this place. There's a river not far away, in walking distance. I just love it."

"Do you? Exactly what do you love about it?"

"The *haus?*"

"*Jah*."

"Everything. It's just in the right location. Close to the bishop's, close to my friend Mary and my other good friend, Beth. It's convenient to everything. There's a huge stove in the kitchen that heats the whole place and a big fireplace in the living room for the winter."

"It really looks small. How many bedrooms?"

"Only the two. But that's one more than I need, so it's plenty."

"Do you keep chickens or anything?"

"I don't. I get my eggs from Beth. She keeps a lot of chickens. And my friend Mary from next door grows enough vegetables for both of us. I really don't get time to look after such things since I'm working all the time."

"And are your friends both married?"

"*Jah,* my two very best friends are. *Denke* for driving me home."

"It was a pleasure. It's the most enjoyable thing I've done all day since meeting you this morning."

She giggled. "I was thinking about that. We must've met before on your previous visits, but I don't remember."

"Me either and I know I would've remembered. Perhaps we didn't meet."

"Maybe not." She got out of the buggy quickly. "I'll see you Monday night."

"*Jah,* I'll see you then."

"Bye, Jason Shroder."

He gave her a big smile and then turned his buggy around and headed away from the house.

She walked inside and then hurried to her bedroom where she looked out the window and saw him trotting the horse and buggy back down the road.

When he was out of sight she flung herself down on her bed, certain that this was the man God had planned for her. The only thing she regretted was taking no mind for her appearance today. Who knew that this ordinary working day might be the day to change her life forever? She'd have to make up for that on Monday night and a new dress was the best way she knew to do it.

She jumped off the bed and pulled her half-made dress out of the cupboard and headed to her treadle sewing machine in the spare room. The main seams were already slip-stitched. She figured she'd be able to get it all finished tonight seeing she wasn't even tired. Meeting Jason had given her a ton of extra energy.

CHAPTER 6

KAREN COULD HARDLY WAIT until her best friends arrived. Their Sunday services were held every other Sunday. And the girls had their regular social get-together at Karen's house on their free Sunday. Since Mary and Beth were married, Karen's house was the ideal place to get together away from men's ears. Karen told her friends all her secrets and feelings and she was sure they told her *nearly* everything.

Mary had a background fairly similar to hers; having also been an only-child, and Beth had just her brother, Samuel, who was Karen's boss and landlord.

Karen stood on the porch waiting to catch a glimpse of Beth's buggy and then she spotted it. The buggy stopped at Mary's house and she watched a small figure hurrying to the buggy. Karen couldn't help but laugh at Mary climbing into the buggy and taking a ride for that short distance rather than walk.

Karen raced into the kitchen, fired up the teakettle and headed back out the door to meet them. She helped secure the buggy horse and then the girls hugged.

"I can't wait to tell you two something. I met a man."

"Who is he?" asked Mary, as she pushed some strands of her red hair back under her *kapp.*

"Tell us everything," Beth said.

"He's the bishop's nephew, Jason. I met him yesterday when I was doing the cleaning with Hannah. He's got the most amazing blue eyes, and he drove me home. And I'm going over to dinner there on Monday night, tomorrow I mean, to the bishop and Hannah's *haus,* and he'll be there too. I think Hannah's going to match us together. You know how she likes to do that."

Mary said, "It's about time you met someone."

"I know. I haven't liked anyone for so long. Anyway, come inside."

They sat in the living room. Karen noticed Mary kept pulling on her sleeve whenever it rode up, and Karen quickly noticed a not-quite-concealed bruise on her friend's arm. This wasn't the first time she'd seen bruises on Mary's pale skin. Mary's husband was a recent convert to the Amish community. Karen knew there was something wrong with the marriage especially since Mary hadn't been her usually happy and bubbly self for some time. It was Karen's fear the bruises were from him. It seemed the only logical explanation. "How's Damian?"

"He's about the same."

She couldn't say anything else if Mary wasn't offering any information. Mary had confided in her before about how bad Damian was, but she'd never mentioned he'd struck her. "And how's William, Beth?"

"He's good. You're looking so well, Karen, you've got a real light to your face. It's like you're lit up from within."

Karen giggled. "I've felt really good since I met Jason and I liked him right away."

Beth said, "Well, I've got some good news too. The doctor said we could start trying again."

Mary squealed. "That's *wonderbaar* news, Beth."

"It's been eight weeks since the last miscarriage and the doctor advised us to wait or we'd surely lose the next one. Now he says that's enough waiting."

Karen said, "We'll pray for a good outcome."

"Denke."

"Jah, we will." Mary tugged at her sleeve once more.

Beth didn't talk about it much now, but when she had first gotten married she used to talk about having at least six children. Six had been her ideal number. Three boys and three girls was what she used to talk about all the time. Now, if she mentioned it, she told the girls she'd be happy with one.

"Did I mention I was going to dinner at the bishops' on Monday night?" Karen asked.

"Only about three times now," Mary said with a laugh.

Karen smiled. "I just can't stop thinking about him."

"Karen, did I tell you Samuel wanted to do some work on the *haus?* The roof needs a little fixing, but Damian told him not to bother."

"Really? Samuel can do some work around here if he wants."

"He didn't come himself. He sent one of his workers to have a look around. Damian's got the idea the bishop sent someone around to spy on him." Mary shrugged her shoulders. "I shouldn't be saying things against Damian, but sometimes it's just so tiring, and I need someone to speak with."

"We understand, Mary. You can talk with us," Beth told her. "Anything you say stops right here.

"Just us friends here. You can tell us anything you want," Karen said. "We know how hard things have been for you."

Mary nodded. "Anyway, let's change the subject. I don't want us to leave here sad. I always feel better after our talks, so let's talk about something happy. I'll put a lot of prayer into my marriage, and then things will surely change."

Beth and Karen nodded.

"We'll both pray for you and Damian, too," said Karen.

Beth turned to Karen, "What you need is a man like my *bruder*. He's done so well. I can't even count the number of houses he has, and three businesses."

Karen giggled thinking about Samuel. He'd done well for himself financially, but he was in his thirties and still unmarried. She'd always found him to be sort of standoffish. "Well, *jah,* someone *like* him," Karen said, being polite for Beth's sake. She couldn't imagine Samuel would be a match with anyone.

"I know what you're thinking. He seems unfriendly but he's not really. He just has a lot on his mind all the time. And he's just so busy all the time, too. I wish he'd slow down."

Karen said, "I wonder why he hasn't sent anyone to my place to have a look at it."

"Perhaps he really is sending someone to spy on my husband for the bishop." Mary pulled a face.

"Jah," Beth said, "surely the bishop has put him up to it."

The three girls laughed.

Karen had so much fun with both of her friends. None of the three of them had the life for which she had hoped. Beth had a happy marriage to William, but unhappiness came to her by way of multiple miscarriages and no children. Mary had no children and an unhappy marriage. And, as for Karen, she was still single. Everyone else they knew seemed so happy. Sometimes it seemed as though they were the three odd ones out in their Amish community.

CHAPTER 7

From Karen's desk at work she could see the comings and goings from the lumberyard's entrance and the parking lot. When she looked up from her bookwork, she saw Jason. He was being stopped by Trevor Yoder, one of the workers. She hurried toward them, wishing she'd taken a little more care over her appearance today.

She heard Trevor say, "He's not here. He rarely visits."

"Doesn't he own this place?" Jason asked.

"*Jah*, he does, but he doesn't run it."

Jason tipped back his hat. "That seems a little odd."

Karen interrupted them, "Hello, Jason. It's nice to see you again. Jason, this is Trevor Yoder. Trevor, this is Jason Shroder."

Trevor nodded, and the men shook hands.

"Ah, the bishop's nephew?" Trevor asked.

"That's right."

"Have a pleasant stay."

"*Denke*. I am so far." Jason looked over at Karen and smiled. Trevor glanced at Karen, and then wandered off. "Do you get a lunch break soon?" Jason asked.

"Not today because I'm working right through my lunch break. I asked to do that so I can leave earlier this afternoon." The way he smiled gave her butterflies. "Were you looking for Samuel just now?"

"Jah, I thought I'd talk to him about a job in one of his companies."

"Like Trevor said, he hardly ever comes here."

Jason's eyebrows drew together. "I thought he'd keep a close eye on his businesses."

"Oh, he does. Believe me. He looks over the books carefully once a week, and keeps a very close eye on the bank balance. Samuel is very particular about his managers."

"I won't interrupt you further. I'll see you tonight, then?"

"Okay."

He turned and headed out of the lot. Suddenly, he turned and hurried back. "Karen, we might not have a chance to speak in private tonight, with a thousand children in the *haus.* Would you come out with me somewhere on Friday night?"

She swallowed hard. Now he was talking about an official date. "I'd like that."

"Good. I'll collect you at say ... six?"

"Okay."

"And how about I collect you from your *haus* this afternoon and take you home again tonight?"

"Denke. That would be ... convenient." She cringed internally when she heard herself say 'convenient.' *Can't you do better than that, Karen?*

He gave her a smile and then strode away. She turned to go back into the building, but glanced at him again. There was purpose in his stride as though he knew where he was heading in life. She found that attractive.

She looked hard and saw him get into his buggy outside the lot. As she walked back into the building, she listened to

36

his horse move away. She'd assumed he'd been teasing her about coming to the lumberyard. Still, it was sweet that he couldn't wait to see her. She didn't really believe he had come there to talk with Samuel, and that was confirmed when he'd asked her about Friday night.

~

KAREN HEADED home with her mind on one thing only, and that was having a long soak in the tub in readiness for her dinner with the Shroders. As her buggy drew closer to home, she was shocked to see a shiny black car parked close to the front door. She had no idea who it could be. Perhaps someone was lost and had the wrong address?

When she stopped the buggy, she saw a man in a dark business suit by her front door. He walked over to her as she got down from the buggy.

"Are you Karen Glick?"

"I am." She felt her heart start racing and hoped she wasn't in some sort of trouble. He looked like he was a lawyer or someone official. "Have I done something wrong?"

He smiled. *"Nee,* not at all. I'm Tim Whitaker. I work for a company that locates heirs who've been left an inheritance. You know you're adopted?"

"I do. What is this about?" Her gaze lowered to a black folder under his arm.

"Were your adoptive parents May Martha Glick and Earnest Benjamin Glick?"

"That's correct, but they're no longer with us."

"I'm sorry to hear that." He took a quick breath. "I have an important matter to discuss with you."

He'd mentioned an inheritance. Had one of her birth parents died? If someone in the community had left her money, she wouldn't be finding out from an *Englischer.*

"Is there somewhere we can talk?" he asked again, looking around. "Can we sit somewhere and discuss everything?"

She was sceptical and wondered suddenly if he was a con man. Although, he didn't look like one. She slipped the buggy reins over the fence. She'd tend to the horse and give him a good rubdown once the man left. Then she turned and took a good look at Mr. Whitaker. He didn't look dangerous. His suit looked too well made for him to need to rob her. And if he were a criminal, he wouldn't have needed to concoct such a story. "Sure. We can sit on the porch."

"Good."

She led the way and sat down on the nearest chair while he took the one furthest away. "What is this about?"

"You have been left an inheritance."

"My parents didn't have anything."

"I'm not talking about your adoptive parents. It's from your grandmother. She left you a sum of money, bypassing her only daughter."

"My grandmother? My real one?" She'd never known the parents of her adoptive parents. They'd all four died before she was born.

"Your birth grandmother, for lack of better terminology."

"That would be my birth mother's mother?"

"Yes."

"Have you met her?"

He shook his head. "No."

"So, she's dead?"

"Your grandmother is, yes."

She was having a little trouble taking it all in. She'd given little thought to her birth parents and zero thought to grandparents being out there, so to speak. "What do you know about her?" She'd never before wanted to know about her mother, but now she was curious.

"I'll fill you in on everything. I must ask you if anyone else comes, can you tell them you have already signed with me?"

It made her uneasy when he mentioned signing something. "What do you mean?"

"I'll need you to sign some documents. You see, we get a small fee for finding you. We only charge an hourly rate and we have a court order in place. Your grandmother nominated us. There are other unscrupulous firms that will charge a percentage such as twenty or thirty percent to do the same as I'm doing, and if you sign with them it will complicate things even though we have the legal rights."

"Oh."

He stared at her. "Okay?"

"Who would come?"

"Another company, like mine, but they'd be ..."

"Yes, I think I understand. You charge by the hour and they charge a percentage, which I'm assuming would work out to a lot more?"

"That's right and If I've been able to find you, then someone else will. And, probably fairly soon. They won't be able to do any more for you than I've done."

That told Karen she'd been easy to find and her mother could've found her if she'd wanted to. "Do I have to pay you any money?"

He chuckled. "No, not at all. Well, it will come out of the inheritance but that's all done thanks to your grandmother. She took care of all that."

"I'll sign." He passed her a paper and she read it carefully. He pulled a pen from his pocket and handed it to her and then she signed the paper at the bottom. Next he passed an identical paper over.

"This copy's for you."

Now she had her grandmother's name, and she should be able to track down her mother.

"You stayed Amish?" he asked.

"I did. I know my birth parents weren't Amish and that's all I know about them."

He folded the paper she had signed and pushed it back into his folder. "I didn't know if I'd be able to find you today, but I'm glad I did." He gave her a beaming smile.

"Where are you from?"

"Richmond, Virginia."

"You came here only to see me?"

"That's right. I'm traveling back tonight."

She looked over at the car. "Driving?"

"That's right. We've got an office there and one in New York. I generally travel between the two."

"Thank you for finding me."

"That's my job. That's what I do."

"What happens now?"

"I need you to come to the office in Richmond to sign some papers and then the money will be wired to your bank account."

"Richmond?"

"I realize it's quite a distance."

"That's where the papers are?"

He nodded.

It was times like these she wished she wasn't alone in life. "And when will I have to do that?"

"The quicker you do it, the quicker your money will come through."

"What's the soonest I can do it, then?"

"I could meet you on Friday at the Richmond office, unless New York is easier for you?"

She knew New York was crowded and she didn't like crowds. "Richmond will be fine."

He pulled out a card from his top jacket pocket, along with the pen. "Meet me in the office at ten o'clock. The money will then be transferred to you, and you should have it the week after."

"That fast?"

"Yes," he said, with his eyes still on his card. Then he circled something on the front of the card and held it out to her. "That's the address there."

She took the card from him. "Thank you. This is all quite unbelievable. I never knew her."

He nodded. "I guessed that. This kind of thing happens all the time. It's not unusual."

"It feels funny that I never knew about her and she knew about me. At least knew of my existence. She must've."

"Correct, she did. There is a letter as well."

"She wrote me a letter?"

"That's right. Do you want to know about your mother?"

"Yes please. I've never met her and I don't know anything about her. It seems funny she wasn't left anything by her own mother."

"In the process of finding you I came across her and met with her. She wants to talk with you. She's asked if you'd meet with her in my office when you come to sign the papers."

"What? Really?"

He nodded.

"I don't know. This is sudden. Tell me about her, please. What do you know?"

"Your mother has been married several times. Four times, I think it was, to wealthy men. That was all stated in the material your grandmother left you."

She wondered how he was able to access something like that. "She's divorced then—my mother?"

"Yes."

"Who's my father? I've never seen my birth certificate. I've been told by my parents there was no father mentioned."

"I don't know about your father. All I know is —"

"How much did my grandmother leave me?"

"Three hundred thousand, nine dollars, and some change."

She gasped. She could buy her own place. Perhaps even buy the cottage from Samuel. "Do you know what my grandmother was like?"

He shook his head. "I just have a name and I can't tell you anything about her." He stood up. "It was nice to meet you, Karen."

"And you." She felt a little rude not asking him in or giving him something to eat before he left, but she had to be mindful she was a single woman. She couldn't ruin her reputation by entertaining an *Englischer* in her home. Her mother had drummed things like that into her. Her mother was extremely mindful of what others might perceive.

WHEN THE MAN LEFT, she hurried to unhitch the buggy and rub down her horse. At this rate, she'd only have time for a quick shower before Jason arrived.

CHAPTER 8

A MILLION THINGS ran through Karen's mind while she was getting ready to go to the bishop's for dinner. She wouldn't get excited about the money until it was hers and then she'd do something sensible with it. Her father had always wanted enough money to own their own home and that's what Karen would do. She knew her parents would be pleased with that wise decision.

After a quick shower, she pulled on her new dress and, after she had finished her hair, she tied her *kapp* and pulled on her stockings and best shoes, and then she waited by the door for Jason. There was something special about wearing a new dress and Karen had a feeling her life was about to take a drastic turn. No longer would she have to live from week to week. Her money worries would be a thing of the past. She closed her eyes and thanked *Gott* for His blessings.

On the tick of six, Jason was in front of the house. She walked out to meet him when he was halfway to the house.

"Hello, Karen. You look lovely. Is that a new dress?"

She giggled, surprised that he'd mentioned her clothes. "It

is fairly new. Did you manage to find Samuel today?" she asked as they both climbed into the buggy.

"Not yet. I was distracted by a few other things. I will talk with him, though. Now, there's something I have to ask you."

"Jah?"

"Do you remember all of Elmer and Hannah's *kinner's* names?"

"Jah. It's easy," Karen said.

He chuckled. "I'm lost. I don't know how you remember them all."

"It helps that I've spent so much time with them, and I've seen their family added to one by one."

"But still … I don't know."

"You'll learn them."

"I'm only here for a week. I'd reckon it'd take six months. I have to keep calling them 'buddy,' or 'my young cousin,' or 'my young friend.' It won't be long before they figure out I don't know their names."

Karen laughed and was pleased how open he was being. "Don't worry. I'm sure you're not the only one who's had that problem. Charles told me the teacher keeps calling him Peter or Aedan."

"Aedan? Is there one called Aedan?"

"Now you're joking with me."

He shook his head and sighed. *"Nee* I'm not."

"I didn't know you were that bad."

He shook his head. "They'll have to wear name tags. Only thing is, then they'll know I don't know their names."

Karen laughed once more and found herself relaxing.

"Our two families aren't that close. Close in miles but not close in *familye* togetherness. Peter and Elmer are close, but my *vadder* was the elder *bruder* by ten years. Peter and Elmer are only separated by one." He continued telling her general things about his family not asking a thing about her life.

When they arrived at the bishop's house, she went in ahead of him while Jason stayed and tended to the horse.

She knocked on the door and walked in to a strangely silent house. "Hello?"

"We're all in here, Karen. Waiting for you."

She walked in and saw the adults and older children at the big table and half a dozen younger children around the smaller table on small chairs. "Oh, are we late?"

"Not by much," the bishop said. "We must have forgotten to name a time for dinner."

"Jason will be in soon."

"Sit by me," Rebecca said. "I've saved you a seat."

Denke. She sat down next to Rebecca and saw from the remaining empty chair that Jason would be seated opposite.

"Can I help, Hannah?"

"Nee." Hannah sat down. "It's all done. Rebecca did most of it."

"I do most of the cooking nowadays and the boys do a lot of the washing up." Karen saw the sad faces on the boys when their sister mentioned the washing up. "Well, someone has to do it. It can't all be me and *Mamm,*" Rebecca told her brothers.

Her mother leaned over and whispered to Rebecca, "You must let others talk at the table."

"Jah, Mamm, I will."

Then Karen heard the sounds of Jason coming in through the back door into the laundry room. Then she heard water running.

"He's washing his hands," one of the boys said.

"Jah, and I hope you all have done the same," the bishop said.

"We have," two of them chorused.

He walked into the room. *"Ach,* sorry. I didn't mean to keep you waiting."

"That's fine. Sit down," Hannah told him, gesturing to the empty chair.

As soon as he sat, everyone closed their eyes for the silent prayer of thanks for the food. Karen could barely contain her excitement at her news and wondered when would be a good time to tell them. Once everyone had food on their plates, she said, "I've had some news today." Everyone turned and looked at her. "It seems my birth-grandmother has died."

"I'm sorry to hear that," Hannah said.

"Does that mean your *mudder* has found you?"

"Nee." She didn't correct Rebecca to say her 'birth *mudder.'* She knew what Rebecca meant. Her "mother" was the woman who raised her. She'd always be her mother in her heart and mind. The two people who raised her were the closest people in the world to her. It had always been the three of them. There were never any siblings, and she'd had all their love and attention. "A man was at my door when I got home from work this afternoon, and he told me my grandmother left me money."

"Have they got the right person?" Hannah asked.

"Jah, he had my name and knew my adoptive parents' names, too."

"Are you going to be rich?" Rebecca asked.

"Rebecca, that's not a polite question."

"Well, I will have more than I had, which was practically nothing. It's not millions, but it's still a large sum. More than I could ever save in a lifetime."

"That's *wunderbaar;* the Lord has blessed you," Bishop Elmer said.

"So, does that mean your *Mamm* is dead?" Rebecca asked.

"Rebecca!" Hannah glared at her daughter.

"I'm sorry. It was just a question. You don't have to answer, Karen."

"I can meet her if I want to. The man who came to my

door said that the money had bypassed the daughter to come directly to me. I asked about my mother and father and he knew nothing much. He told me a little that he knew about my mother. At first, I thought the man was going to ask for money, I mean, it was quite the unbelievable story. But, he didn't and I think it's all true."

"When will you get the money?" Rebecca asked. When her mother glared at her again, she said, "I'm only asking, *Mamm*."

"I have to go to somewhere in Richmond and sign some papers."

"In person?" Hannah asked.

"*Jah*."

"Why couldn't they post the papers?" Jason asked.

Karen shrugged her shoulders. It didn't occur to her to ask. "I don't know. He didn't suggest it."

"And you have to do that soon?" the bishop asked.

"He said as soon as I can. As soon as I do that, the money is wired to me."

"Will you find out anything about your parents?" Timothy asked.

"I've never been curious before. Because I figured they gave me up. And it doesn't matter what the circumstances were. I'm not angry with them or anything, I just don't have any feelings for them."

"Why not?" Rebecca asked. "Aren't you cranky with your *mudder*? She gave you away."

"*Nee*. Your *vadder* once told me it's not important where you've been It's where you're going that's important. And, *Gott* willing, I know where I'm going." Karen smiled at Rebecca.

Rebecca looked over at her father and then looked back at Karen. "You must be curious, though. Don't you wonder if you look like somebody in your family?"

"I don't really think about it. Or at least I didn't. But now it all seems real. From time to time I wondered what my parents were like, but I never dwelt on it. I never thought of the grandparents I might have had."

When Rebecca opened her mouth, her mother said, "Remember what I said before this dinner began, Rebecca?"

"Jah, Mamm. I'm dominating the conversation."

"That's right, and if you say one more word, I'll have you sit at the children's table for a week."

Rebecca looked down at her food.

The bishop said, "Have you given any thought to how you'd get to Richmond?"

"Nee, it's only just happened tonight."

"Jason, since you're not working, why don't you accompany Karen to Richmond?"

Karen froze in place and couldn't believe her ears. It would be a perfect opportunity to get to know him better. She glanced at Jason and saw him grinning.

Jason looked at the bishop, making no attempt to hide his delight. "I'd be happy to, *Onkel.* What do you say, Karen?"

"I can't put you to all the trouble."

"I'm not doing anything else. Anyway, I've never been to Richmond. I wouldn't mind seeing a bit more of the country."

"Very good, it's settled then, and I'll send Aunt Agatha with the both of you."

Karen's heart sank.

"Wait, what? Aunt Agatha?" Jason asked the bishop.

"Jah, you know that two unmarried people can't travel alone."

It had been too good to be true that they be sent somewhere without a chaperone. Aunt Agatha was the Bishop's old aunt. Karen guessed she'd be ninety.

"Do you think she'd be okay to travel the distance?" Jason asked.

"Jah, she's strong. She'll outlive us all. She's not really like any other ninety-three-year-old, she's more like seventy."

Jason said, "Whatever you say. Would you like to have me make travel inquiries, Karen?"

"Nee, I'll make the arrangements," the bishop said.

"Denke," Karen said. "I'll have to be at work early tomorrow and I'll tell them I'll need a couple of days off."

"Call me tomorrow and let me know if you need me to talk to Samuel for you," said Bishop Elmer.

LATER THAT NIGHT when Jason was driving Karen home, he said, "I'm sorry about our Friday night. It's not going to be the same with Aunt Agatha, but we'll make the most of it."

She giggled. "That was a bit of a surprise."

"It was, but hopefully we'll have a few quiet moments away from Aunt Agatha, if you want."

"That would be nice."

"She's really not bad for an old lady."

"Oh, I know. I like her. Everyone in the community calls her Aunt Agatha whether they're related to her or not. She probably is related to three quarters of the community come to think of it." She smiled at him and then quickly got out of the buggy, so they wouldn't have the awkward silent moment. *"Denke* for the ride home."

"I'll pick you up nice and early on Thursday morning. It'll be an early start, I'd dare say. Anyway, I'll let you know ahead of time as soon as *Onkel* Elmer has booked everything."

"That would be great." She turned and walked to the door, and while she did so, he turned the buggy around.

CHAPTER 9

THE NEXT NIGHT AFTER WORK, Karen pulled up her horse and buggy at Beth's place. There was only one friend she could visit because she never liked visiting Mary unannounced in case Damian was there. She didn't trust him. There was something wrong about him. He was friendly and everything on the outside but Mary told her a different story about his actions.

Beth ran out to meet her as soon as she'd stopped the buggy. "Karen, is everything okay?"

"Jah, why wouldn't it be?"

"We never see each other on a weekday. It's always the weekend."

Karen jumped down from the buggy. "I have exciting news to tell you."

"About Jason?"

"Kind of, but something else exciting happened. Is William home?"

"Nee, he's not home for another hour."

"Do you have time to talk?"

"Jah, come inside and tell me all your exciting news."

She couldn't wait to get inside; she started talking as they walked. "When I arrived home from work yesterday there was a car."

"Outside your *haus?*"

Karen nodded. "There was a car and there was a man in a suit. His name was Tim Whitaker and he'd come to tell me that my grandmother had died."

"Your biological grandmother?"

"Jah."

"Does that mean your parents have been in touch with you?"

"Nee, they haven't. But this man contacted me because my grandmother left me money."

"She must've known where you were all this time."

"That's just it. Tim had to track me down to find me, so I don't think she knew where I was. She gave him—his firm, the job to find me after she died."

"Well, you must have been on her mind all these years and she must've known that her daughter or son had you."

"It was my mother's mother. He told me a bit about my mother. I don't think she and my grandmother got along because she didn't leave any money to her."

"That's interesting."

"Tim said my mother had been married a few times to wealthy men."

"Then she's probably got a bit of money of her own and she might never need the money."

"That's what I thought. Anyway, I have to travel to sign papers to get the money and the bishop said Jason could go with me."

"Really? He allowed that?"

Karen giggled. "You won't believe it. He actually suggested it. There's only one catch. Aunt Agatha will be traveling with us."

Beth laughed along with her. "I didn't think it sounded right. It won't really be the same."

"I know. But still, I'll get to be close to him for a couple of days."

"When do you have to go to sign the papers?"

"On Friday. And we're leaving Thursday morning and staying overnight Thursday and Friday, then we'll be back Saturday evening. I hope I don't have to share a room with Agatha. She probably snores." The two girls giggled.

"I'm so pleased for you. Is it a lot of money?"

"A fair amount. A little over three hundred thousand."

"Wow! That's a fortune. You'll be set for life."

"I know."

"Tell me what happened with Jason last night at the dinner."

A little giggle escaped Karen's lips. "He came to my work at lunchtime hoping we could have lunch, but I'd already asked the manager if I could work through my break to get off a little earlier because of the dinner invitation. He joked about stopping by the lumberyard. At least, I thought it was a joke. Anyway, while he was there, he asked me out for Friday night."

"Wow, things are going so well for you."

"But now we'll be traveling on the train instead."

"At least he asked you. That's a good sign. So many good things are happening for you. What have you been doing differently?"

Karen rubbed her forehead. "Nothing."

"Have you been praying more?"

"Just the same amount."

Beth let out a huge sigh. "I was hoping you would have some formula for having your prayers answered."

"*Nee*, I can't think of anything I've done differently." She knew her friend was thinking about all the miscarriages she'd had and was looking for some kind of 'prayer formula.' "I'll go now, before William comes home."

"Okay, I'll have exciting news to tell him. Am I allowed to tell him?"

"Jah, it's no secret. Can you believe it? I'll have enough to buy a *haus.* I am going to ask Samuel if I can buy the cottage I'm living in."

"You want me to ask him for you?"

"Ach nee, Beth. For a minute there, I forgot he's your *bruder."*

"I don't mind asking him."

"Nee, please don't. This is something I need to do by myself. I just want to ask him if he has been thinking of selling it; then I would like to buy it. If you ask him, he might be obliged to sell it to me and I don't want him to feel that. Save it for when I need a real favor."

"Like a few days off work?"

"I've already asked for Thursday and Friday off work. I just had to ask my manager for that."

"And how is your manager?"

"He's very easy to get along with. He gave me the time off with no questions asked."

"You're a good worker."

Karen slowly nodded. "I hope so."

"You are, or you wouldn't be working for Samuel."

Karen smiled at her friend. Beth's brother had the reputation of being hard, but fair.

CHAPTER 10

THE DAYS FLEW BY, and Karen looked out the window at eight o'clock on Thursday morning to see Jason pulling up in a taxi. It was a little over nine and a half hours on the train one way, and the bishop had booked motel rooms for the three of them.

Karen picked up her bag with her few changes of clothing and when she opened the door, she was faced with Jason.

"Let me take that for you." He reached down and took the bag out of her hand.

"Denke." She looked over into the taxi and saw Aunt Agatha. "Aunt Agatha didn't mind going?"

"She said she's looking forward to it. She's visited Richmond before but not for a long time. She said she's going to catch up with a few friends."

"Oh, that's surprising."

"Aunt Agatha is a woman who's full of surprises."

"I don't doubt it." Karen closed the door behind her and the two headed to the taxi.

ON THE TRAIN, Karen sat opposite Aunt Agatha and Jason sat beside Aunt Agatha. Karen had little legroom as Aunt Agatha's legs were stretched out with no thought for Karen.

After a little small talk was had, Jason spent some time looking out the window.

Soon Aunt Agatha fished into her bag and pulled out some knitting.

"What are you knitting?" Karen asked.

"I'm knitting squares. Our ladies' knitting circle is knitting squares, nine inches by nine inches, and we're making blankets with them."

"For?" Jason asked, momentarily taking his eyes off the passing scenery.

"We're auctioning them off at the charity auction. You should come."

"Why's that ... I mean, when is it?" he asked.

"On the ninth."

"I might be still around by then. Who knows?" He smiled at Karen. And she looked away not wanting Aunt Agatha to get any inkling they liked each other.

"Do you knit, Karen?" Agatha asked.

Karen dreaded it when the older ladies in the community asked whether she knitted or sewed. There was only one reason they asked and she didn't have time to join groups. "Not very well," she parroted her usual answer to those kinds of questions.

"You need more practice then. You should come join our knitting circle."

"Karen works," Jason said.

"In my day, young girls didn't work so much."

"Things were probably different back then. If my parents were still alive I probably wouldn't need to work so much, but as you know, they aren't."

"In my day, a young woman like you would be married. How old are you?"

"Older than most single women, I suppose. Left on the shelf, and such, and ... what not." She found it much easier if she said things like that before others pointed it out.

"Everyone's an individual," said Jason, trying to help her out.

Aunt Agatha's body swiveled to face him. "And what's your excuse for not being married, Jason?"

He stared at his aunt with big blue eyes. "I run way too fast."

She smiled and looked back at her knitting. "You're just like your *vadder*, David ... Elmer ... I mean, Jason. But jokes will only get you so far. You need to be more serious about life."

"I'm working on it, Aunt Agatha. And, the name's Jason."

She ignored him about the name mix up. "And so you should be. And Hannah tells me you don't even have a job at the moment."

Jason opened his blue eyes wide. "And just as well. Who would've accompanied you two ladies and kept you both out of trouble?"

She smiled at him and then looked across at Karen. "I don't think we'd get into any trouble, would we, Karen?"

"We'll never find out now with Jason around." She swallowed hard suddenly becoming nervous. "I want to thank both of you for coming with me. It would've been awful to do this by myself."

"It was a pleasure, dear," Agatha said.

"It's exciting," Jason said. "You never know what you'll find out."

"About my parents?"

"*Jah,* where you came from and such and what your family is like."

"I've never been interested. I suppose it is unusual not to know anything."

Out of the blue, Aunt Agatha said, "Elmer said he booked a double room for us, Karen."

"Oh, okay." It was her worst fear. She'd never be able to relax. And she just knew Agatha would snore.

It wasn't long before Agatha had her head leaning back and her mouth wide open. Her hands were still clasped onto her knitting. Jason and Karen stifled giggles every time they looked at her.

Jason leaned over and said quietly, "You didn't look too happy about sharing a room. Do you want a separate room from Aunt Agatha?"

"I did, but it would cost more and I don't have my money through yet."

"I'll talk to the clerk when we get there."

"Really? Do you think you could change it?"

"I'll see what I can do. It's not a popular night of the week, so you never know."

WHEN THEY FINALLY REACHED THE motel after their long train ride, Agatha suddenly had to use the rest room even though she had used the one at the train station.

Jason went in to get the keys from the office while Karen waited in the lobby outside the ladies restroom until Aunt Agatha was finished.

"Do we have the keys yet?" Agatha came out of the restroom drying her hands on a white handkerchief.

"Jason's gone to get them."

"I can't wait to lie down and rest my weary bones. I don't know why traveling takes so much out of a person. We were sitting down the whole time, so what's so tiring?"

"That's very true. It is just one of those strange things."

"Let's find Jason. He shouldn't be taking this long." Agatha took off at quite a pace and Karen stayed behind her. They walked up to the office area, and Jason walked out before they got there with a single set of keys in his one hand and dangling two sets in the other.

"The manager was kind enough to give us three separate rooms for tonight. Tomorrow, you two will have to share."

Aunt Agatha looked horrified. "That wasn't the arrangement. I was supposed to be sharing with. Jane ... Janet ... Karen."

Karen frowned, wondering where she'd gotten those other names from but even more concerned that Agatha would insist on sharing. "Wouldn't you like a nice room of your own, Aunt Agatha? I mean, it's not as though Jason and I are going to sneak off anywhere together."

"Oh, we would never do anything like that." Jason shook his head.

"Ach nee. I didn't think you were going to do something like that. It's just that ... that's what the arrangements were."

Jason stared at her again with his innocent blue eyes. "It's no problem, Aunt Agatha. If you really want to share I'll just have the manager change you both back to sharing a room."

"Don't bother yourself with that now. Just give me the key."

A little smile tugged at the corners of his lips as Aunt Agatha took the key from his outstretched hand.

CHAPTER 11

AFTER A QUICK AND easy dinner at one of the local cafés, they retired to their own rooms, but not before Agatha once again reminded them she wouldn't be there the next day, but she'd be back by evening.

Karen unlocked her door and stepped into the room. It seemed clean enough. A double bed took up most of the room and there was space for only one nightstand beside the bed. She pushed open the door of the ensuite bathroom. It was all she needed, just a toilet, hand basin and shower. It didn't matter what the room was like, she was grateful she wouldn't be sharing tonight.

Karen placed her bag onto her bed, pulled out a nightie and headed to the shower. The train trip had been nearly as exhausting as making polite small talk over dinner with Jason's great aunt. It seemed she thought she'd been sent with them to challenge everything either of them said.

As the hot water poured pulsating jets of water down onto Karen's back, it struck her as odd that her life was about to change so much. Two weeks ago, she had no idea Jason existed and now he was traveling with her on the most important journey of her life.

The only nagging doubt she had about Jason was that he might be an unsettled kind of man. A man who always had itchy feet, having trouble settling in one place. Karen didn't want to leave her community, nor did she want to move from place to place while he looked for a job.

After her shower, she had the option of using the electricity to run the air conditioning. At home on a hot night all she could do was open the windows and place a cold flannel cloth on her forehead. She flicked on the power for the air conditioner and then leaped under the covers and closed her eyes.

THE NEXT THING she knew there was loud knocking on her door. She woke up in darkness and felt as though it was the middle of the night. "Karen."

"*Jah*, Jason?"

"You were meeting me for breakfast. Remember?"

She rubbed her eyes. "What time is it?"

Through the closed door, he replied, "It's a quarter to eight and you said you'd meet me at seven thirty."

"I'm coming. Just give me ten minutes." She couldn't even open the door slightly because he would have seen her without a prayer *kapp*.

"Okay, I'll be waiting right here."

With that extra pressure on her, she laid out her clothes and then hurried to the bathroom to clean her teeth and do her hair.

In double-quick time, she was ready. Before she walked out to meet him, she had a quick look in the bathroom mirror. Deciding she looked okay, she headed to the door and opened it with a smile.

"Sleep in?" he asked.

"*Jah,* it was the curtains. I didn't realize how they would block the light. Oh, the air conditioner. I should turn it off " She went back inside to turn it off.

He came right up to the doorway. "Grab your things. You're checking out of this room today, remember?"

"That's right." She threw her belongings into her bag; he took it from her and locked it in his room.

"There." He turned to face her. "I hear there's a place two doors up that makes the most amazing breakfasts. You hungry?"

"I'm starving. What about Aunt Agatha?"

"She's already left. I saw her hurrying down the road a few minutes ago."

They walked into the coffee shop and ordered two large breakfasts of bacon, eggs and hash browns.

"It's just the two of us now, so far from home," he said.

"It's quite unbelievable. I only met you just days ago and here we are taking a trip together."

He leaned forward. "Carefully chaperoned by Aunt Agatha."

She nodded. How could she forget?

"Do you know where we're going today?"

"I have the address. It's ten minutes by taxi. Not too far. *Denke* for coming with me."

"You can stop thanking me. I'm glad to do it. And I wasn't doing anything else exciting. Anyway, I can't think of anything I'd rather be doing right now." He gave her a big smile. "Have you thought about what you're going to do with the money?"

"I'm not too sure just yet. It still doesn't seem real. And I keep thinking that something is going to block it at the last minute."

"Something or someone? You know there might be people who are out to contest the will?"

"What do you mean?"

"They can take you to court if they feel they should have gotten the money rather than you."

"Jah. I have had that in the back of my mind and I'm hoping it won't happen. I guess that's why I'm not feeling too excited about it until I actually have it."

"I guess that's a good way to be. And you'll meet your mother today."

"I'm scared about that."

"Why?"

"For so many reasons. I don't know why she couldn't keep me. Or maybe she could and just didn't want to. I've thought of little else the last few days. I've come up with hundreds of reasons she got rid of me."

"You'll soon know the truth. Anyway, it's her story, not yours. You know who you are already and where you're going. You're a child of *Gott.*"

She smiled and nodded. It was just what his Uncle Elmer, the bishop, would've said. And it helped to quiet her mind.

CHAPTER 12

AFTER THEIR BREAKFAST, Jason and Karen took a taxi to the address on Tim Whitaker's business card and ended up in front of a three-story building.

Karen took a deep breath. "Here I go." She took another look at the card. "Second floor."

"Do you want me to wait out here?"

"Why don't you sit in the coffee shop?" She pointed to the coffee shop on the ground floor. "I don't know how long I'll be. I can't imagine I'd have much to say to my mother."

"Will you be okay?"

"*Jah*, I think so. I just have to sign papers and that's it. And meet my mother, but that won't take hours. Not if she wanted to meet me here."

"Okay. I'll see you soon. Don't hurry on my account. Take your time."

She left him and went up in the elevator to find Tim's office. When the doors opened she realized the whole floor was office space for Tim's firm. She'd expected a few rooms, not the whole floor. The woman behind the desk in front of her looked up and Karen walked forward.

"I'm looking for Tim Whitaker."

"Do you have an appointment?"

"Yes, I'm Karen Glick."

"Have a seat. He won't be long."

She looked over at the side where the woman pointed, walked across and sat down on one of the two couches in the waiting area.

Once Tim was striding toward her and smiling, she felt much better. "You made it."

"I did." She stood.

"This way. We're waiting for you in the boardroom."

She gulped. "We?"

"The lawyer."

"Oh." She then whispered, "When will I meet my mother?"

"She should be here shortly."

She followed him into a room where a man was sitting at a table. He jumped up to shake her hand and introduced himself as Warwick Baker. *Warwick? What were his parents thinking, to give a baby boy that name?*

"I'll go through the whole procedure with you," Baker said.

A large knot formed in her stomach as she sat down. Had it been a mistake to come up here alone? She thought she could be independent but now she wished she had someone with her. After Warwick had explained everything he push the papers forward for her to sign.

"Put your signature there next to the X and the money will be wired into your account."

She took the pen and stopped just before she touched the paper. "When should I expect the money?"

"It should hit your account in a day or two. Keep in mind the weekend holds things up and it's already into Friday, so I'd say by the middle of next week."

"Good." She looked down and signed the papers.

The lawyer handed over a business card. "Here's my number if you have any questions." Then he gave her a large envelope with a copy of everything and was gone.

She turned to Tim. "Thank you for finding me. Is there any way I can find out about my grandmother other than from my mother?"

He opened the folder and pulled out a letter. "She left you this."

"That's right. I forgot about the letter."

When he handed it to her she stared at the white envelope with simply the name Karen on the front. The envelope wasn't sealed and it was crinkled as though a hundred people had opened it already.

"You don't have to read it now," he said.

"I won't, thank you. I'll read it later."

A woman came into the room and whispered something to Tim. When she went out, Tim turned to her. "Your mother's here. Are you ready to meet her?"

Something about meeting in a lawyer's office seemed cold and unfriendly. A park or some gardens would've been nicer, if this woman couldn't see fit to invite her daughter to her home. "I am." Once again, her heart pumped hard as she followed him into another office.

"Wait in here," he said nodding his head.

Once she was seated, a fiftyish woman, who looked equally as nervous as Karen felt, walked into the room.

CHAPTER 13

KAREN'S biological mother just stared at her and Karen wondered what she thought. The woman was tall with a slender build and she wore a figure-hugging pale blue jacket with a matching skirt. Her facial features were attractive and she enhanced them with quite a generous application of make-up. Her platinum blonde hair was piled on top of her head and large diamonds flashed from her earlobes.

Karen stood up, wondering if they should embrace or something, but then the woman sat down with not even an extended hand.

"They told me you went to an Amish settlement. I was able to approve some couples and I approved three. I let the social worker have the final choice."

Karen was horrified; someone this woman didn't know had the final say on who would raise her?

"You stayed with the Amish I see."

"I did." It was like talking with a total stranger. Almost more awkward, Karen thought. Maybe her father would be different. "Can I ask you about my father?"

"He was no one important. He was my first husband. He's

dead now. I was moving on to my second, and you were ... in the way, to put it bluntly. You wouldn't have fitted into my life. I couldn't take care of a child and that's the truth."

"Did my father know about me? When did he die?"

"He died about ten years ago. And, no, he didn't know about you, ever. I had to go away for a while when I separated from him."

She was cold and distant and Karen hoped that her grandmother hadn't been like that. "Can you tell me anything about my grandmother?"

"She was a vicious old cow."

Karen was taken aback. "That's your mother you're talking about."

"You asked and I told you. She left you money to spite me. It just goes to show who she was."

"You can have the money if you want it."

She turned up her nose. "That money is just small change to me. Keep it since she wanted you to have it."

She wondered how much money her mother had if the inheritance was small change. "Can I ask why you wanted to see me?"

"I thought it was the right thing to do since you were going to be in town."

"You live here?"

"Of course."

The two women stared at one another. Karen was pleased she had been raised by her loving parents, May and Earnest Glick. "Have you thought much about me over the years?"

"On and off."

Karen felt bad because she didn't feel anything for the woman at all. It was a disappointment, but it was a cold, hard fact.

"How long are you staying?" her mother asked.

"I'm going back in the morning."

"I suppose you should give me your home address."

"Sure, if you give me yours."

"Yes, of course." She pulled out a notebook from her bag and scribbled an address on it and ripped it out and gave it to Karen. Then she handed the book over to Karen with the pen. "Write your name and address in here. I see they didn't change the name I gave you."

"You named me?"

"I did. I named you after your grandmother when we were still getting along. Her name was Karina. I chose the more normal name of Karen."

Karen knew she'd probably never see the woman again. "And what is your name?"

"Maggie Briggs."

She tried to remember all the questions she'd thought of. "How long did you have me before you gave me away?"

"That's a cold way to put it."

"Oh? How would you say it?"

"I adopted you out to give you a better life than you would've had if you'd stayed. You would've been raised by nannies, and I would have been no good to you as a mother."

"And how long did you keep me?" Karen asked again.

"Five days."

After she processed the answer to that question, she asked another. "Do I look like my father?"

"A little. Well, it was nice to meet you finally, I mean, again."

"And you."

The woman leaned over, putting her arm lightly around Karen's shoulders, and leaned in for a token hug, and then she pulled away quickly. "Goodbye."

"Goodbye," Karen said softly, wishing she felt something from, and for, Maggie Briggs.

KAREN SAT THERE ALONE for a few moments. Some of her questions had been answered. She was a little sad her father never knew of her existence. She stared at the address Maggie had given her and wondered if she'd ever see the woman again. When she glanced up at the clock on the wall, she saw that better than half an hour had passed since she'd entered the building. She must've been with her birth mother for much longer than it seemed.

KAREN LEFT the lawyer's office and found Jason sitting at the back of the coffee shop reading a newspaper. She sat down in front of him placing the file she'd been given on the table.

"How did the meeting with your mother go?"

"It was a bit awful. She called her own mother an old cow."

He nodded slowly, sympathy in his eyes. "I'm sorry it wasn't what you hoped for."

She sighed. "I'm not sure what I'd hoped for. I never felt I wanted to meet her, not until this whole grandmother thing came up. I would've liked to meet her, my grandmother, I think. Now I never can."

"You have the answers, you have the family of God, the community where you have your earthly home. Just because she's your mother doesn't mean you're anything like her."

She knew he was right, but she couldn't stop the tears from falling. "Oh, I don't know why I'm crying now. I didn't even feel like crying upstairs."

He passed her a napkin. "It's the suddenness of it all. Just let yourself cry."

Once he said that, she no longer felt the need to cry. "I've got the letter from my grandmother."

"You read it?"

"Not yet. I might read it tonight. *Nee*, I might read it now if you don't mind waiting a few more moments."

"I'm fine. It's nearly midday. Why don't we just stay here for lunch?"

"Okay." She opened the letter and the first thing she noticed was the delightful handwriting. It was the writing of an old person, neat and with scrolls on each of the capital letters.

Dear Karen,

The last time I saw you was when you were two days old. I held you in my arms and tried to talk your mother into keeping you, but she wouldn't hear of it. I wish and hope that you have had a good life. If you are reading this, that means I have gone to my maker.

Karen had to stop because the tears were threatening to come back. She reminded herself she didn't even know this person and forced herself to continue reading.

I didn't do a good job raising your mother and one day I might realize what I did wrong. The money in my will is my way of saying I have always thought about you and you have always been in my heart. As my granddaughter, you've always been a part of me. I wish you the best.

Your loving grandmother,
Karina

EVEN THOUGH SHE had never thought about her grandmother's existence, it made her feel good and special that the woman held her close to her heart. Now she felt she could share that with Jason. She looked up at him.

"How was it?"

"It was nice. It was lovely to read that after meeting my mother. This letter has made me feel someone cared about me."

"I'm glad."

She folded the letter and placed it down on the table and stared at it. That letter had been held in her grandmother's own hands.

"Are you ready to eat?"

She nodded and smiled. "It seems we're always eating." She noticed him look at the letter. "Do you want to read it?"

Jason smiled at her. "Would you mind?"

Karen passed the letter over, pleased he wanted to read it.

He read it, and said, "You're right. That's nice," as he passed it back.

"I know. It makes me happy that she's been thinking of me even though I don't even know anything about her except her name."

"How old were you when you found out you were adopted?"

"They told me when I was around five. They didn't want me to find out from anybody else at school. I had no idea what adopted meant." She laughed as she remembered her parents explaining it to her.

"It would be quite a shock for someone to learn it from someone other than their parents."

She nodded. "I never felt any different except my parents were a lot older than my friends' parents. That and the fact that I was an only child. That's quite rare in our community."

He passed her a menu. "I wonder how Aunt Agatha's doing."

"I'd say she'd be having a good time wherever she is."

CHAPTER 14

AFTER THEY SPENT the rest of the afternoon looking around the area, Karen and Jason decided they'd have a rest in their separate rooms while waiting for Aunt Agatha to return.

Karen knocked on the door to the room where Agatha and she were to spend the night together. There was no answer, so Karen got a spare key from the office, opened tbe door, walked in and kicked off her shoes. She lay on one of the single beds hoping Agatha wouldn't be home before dinner like she'd said. That would leave her and Jason to have a quiet dinner by themselves. A few minutes later, Karen's hopes were dashed when she heard a key jiggling in the lock.

Agatha walked into the room. "Oh, I'm sorry. I didn't wake you up, did I?"

Karen sat up. *"Nee*, I just got in a few minutes ago."

"What are we doing for the evening meal?"

"We're meeting Jason in about an hour if that's all right."

"Suits me. It will give me time to have a little lie down." Agatha lay down on the bed without taking off her shoes. Two minutes later she was snoring.

Karen stifled giggles. Somehow, she'd known Agatha was a snorer. After that, Karen must've drifted off to sleep because the next thing she knew there was a knock on the door. She opened her eyes and sat up to see Agatha sitting up on her bed and reading her bible.

"That must be Jason," Agatha said, closing the book with a finger marking the page.

Karen quickly sat up and by the time Agatha opened the door, Karen was on her feet.

"Is everyone ready?" Jason asked.

"Do either of you mind if I don't join you?" Agatha asked.

Jason asked, "You're not feeling ill, are you, Aunt Agatha?"

"Not at all. I've been visiting people all day, and with social visits always comes plenty of food. I don't think I can fit another thing in until tomorrow."

Karen hoped she wasn't smiling too much.

"I think Karen and I could manage by ourselves," Jason said managing to keep a straight face.

Agatha waved a finger at him. "Just you be sure to have her back here by nine o'clock."

Karen's gaze flickered to the digital clock on the night-stand between the two single beds. It was already six. That gave them three hours of alone time.

"I'll have her back here by nine. Don't worry."

"Very good." She wagged a finger at him. "And if you don't, I'll have to tell *Onkel* Elmer."

He chuckled. "I'll be extra certain to have her back, in that case."

Karen walked through the door and Agatha closed it behind them. It was like a breath of fresh air to be alone with Jason once again. They walked side-by-side in the fresh evening air, heading away from the motel.

"Where shall we go for dinner?" she asked.

"Why don't we go for a little walk and see what we find?"

"Okay." They walked a few more paces. "Aunt Agatha makes a good chaperone."

Jason chuckled. "She does. I thought she'd be looking over our shoulders the whole time."

"Me too. Are you hungry?"

"I don't know. I think so. I ate while I was waiting for you and again when you came back, but I can always eat. I've been giving it some thought and I think I remember your mother and father. May, and Earnest, is that right?"

"Yeah, that's them. What do you remember about them?"

"Your *vadder* was tall with a long gray beard and your mother was small and always had a smile on her face. He was an elder, *jah?*"

"He was."

"I didn't visit your community often when I was a child, and I don't really know why because our communities are fairly close. I think it was because my *vadder* doesn't like to travel and his brothers traveled to see him instead."

Karen nodded. "People just get busy with their own lives and it's hard to know where the time goes sometimes."

"I know. I woke up one day and realized all my friends were married and I was the only one left."

"How old were you then?" Karen asked.

"Twenty-four, I guess, and that was four years ago. It just never happened and I'm not sure why. Maybe I never met the right woman."

"Maybe." She was pleased he was the same age.

"Until now." He turned toward her and gave her a big smile

She smiled back at him and didn't know what to say. When she noticed they were outside a diner, she said, "This place looks good."

"Okay." When they sat in the only spare booth, Jason said, "Order what you want. My treat."

"Nee, my treat. I just inherited a lot of money, remember?"

"I insist. You have to save that money and do something practical with it."

She gave a little giggle. "That's exactly what my *vadder* would've said."

"And he was right."

"Okay, you win."

"Good. And now we've got over that hurdle, since you missed our Friday night date how about we make it this coming Friday instead?"

She was pleased he hadn't forgotten. "That suits me fine, but isn't this Friday ... hmm?"

He pressed his lips together and shook his head. His blue eyes were sparkling with mischief all the while. "It's not the same."

"Okay."

"Good." He passed her one of the menus, and then read through the other.

After a while, Karen said, "I'll have the chilli dog and barbeque ribs."

He stared at her. "Really?"

"Jah, why?"

"That's just what I was going to order, only with fries. We're so similar."

After the waitress took their order, Karen's mind drifted back to Maggie Briggs. "It's hard to believe I've finally met my mother after all these years."

"Jah, it would be weird."

"I just wish she wasn't so cold."

Jason said, "Maybe she's protecting herself from her feelings. It can't be easy to give away a child."

"Maybe, maybe not. Some women just don't like children. She said something about me being in the way of her living her own life."

"It's possible she's one of that kind." He shrugged his shoulders. "I guess."

"All I know is she didn't get along with my grandmother and my father is dead. I have all the names on the family tree in the paperwork that Tim gave me. So, I could look up my relatives if I wanted to."

"When ... or why would you do that?"

"I thought about it, but my *familye* is the *familye* of *Gott*, isn't it?"

He nodded. "Exactly. That's your important *familye*. You don't need to find anyone else if you don't feel you should."

She was grateful for his support. "I've been so wound up with my own problems I haven't even had a chance to ask you how things are with you."

He frowned at her. "In what way?"

"Looking for work."

He gave a low chuckle as though that had been the last thing on his mind. "I've been helping *Onkel* Peter a little bit and haven't done much about my job search."

She was disappointed to hear that. He seemed rather unmotivated. "You think you should put a plan in place?" Karen hoped she wasn't crossing the line of their friendship, but she had to find out what made him tick.

"A plan to do what?"

"A plan to get a job."

"I'm in no particular hurry. I'll just see what presents itself."

Karen was glad when the waitress brought their drinks and interrupted their conversation. Karen didn't understand his lack of work ethic and to her that was a serious problem.

The rest of the evening with Jason was enjoyable. Karen made sure they kept off the topic of employment. Their leisurely stroll back to the motel under the moonlight was romantic. For Karen, it was a welcome change to feel wanted by a man, but she wasn't going to get carried away too fast and live to regret it.

CHAPTER 15

W HEN K AREN WALKED into the motel room she saw Agatha
sitting up in bed still reading the bible.

"Agatha, have you been reading this whole time?"

"It's nine already?"

"A few minutes before nine."

"How did things go for you?"

She stared at Aunt Agatha wondering what she meant.
"With Jason?"

"*Jah.* I noticed something going on between you two.
Some funny business, and I know that's why Elmer suggested
that he come out here with us."

"Funny business?" It was then that Karen knew Agatha
didn't know she was the chaperone. She thought Jason was
tagging along with the two of them.

"There's something between the two of you, is there not?"
Agatha blinked rapidly.

"Wait, what was the question?" Karen asked.

"How are things between the two of you? You and Jason?"

"Really good. We get along really well."

"That is good to hear. It makes sense the two of you found each other. You're both in your twenties and unmarried."

"So, because of our similar ages you think that makes us a match?"

"Well, you both get along, don't you?"

"We do."

"Then it's pretty obvious that the two of you should marry."

Karen sat heavily on her bed and proceeded to untie her shoelaces. "Besides the fact that he hasn't asked me, wouldn't I need to make sure he's the right man for me?"

"At your age, you can't be too fussy. And I'm not telling you that to be rude. If you don't marry Jason, where is the next single man your age coming from? His family lives close by and that is convenient. Unless you want to travel to find another man? But, I'd wager he'd wouldn't be as good as Jason is."

Karen stifled a giggle at the prim and proper woman taking about a wager. She'd never say that in front of her nephew, the bishop. That aside, she was starting to see the practical side of Aunt Agatha. "I know, but I just want to have a really good and happy marriage. I don't want there to be any problems down the road."

"Oh, my dear girl. What problems could there be if you both have your eyes fixed on the Lord?"

Karen's mind traveled to Mary's sad marriage. She'd entered into that marriage full of love and hope and now it was falling down around her. "You think I could marry anybody who is around my age and the marriage would be successful?"

"*Jah.* If both your eyes are on *Gott.*"

There was something seriously wrong with so simplistic an answer as that. Karen tried to show her a different side of things by presenting the opposite viewpoint in the subtlest way she could. "I know there are some people in the community whose marriages are happier than others. I just want to make sure mine is one of the happier ones."

"And it will be if you make it so," Agatha stated firmly.

If only it were that easy, and something told Karen it wasn't. She couldn't tell Aunt Agatha about Mary's marriage, so she kept quiet. "We'll just have to wait and see if Jason asks me, then." She only said that to keep Agatha happy.

"He'd be a fool if he didn't. Well, I'm going to get ready for bed."

After Aunt Agatha had the longest shower in the history of mankind, Karen used the bathroom for a quick shower and was surprised there was hot water left.

When she came out of the bathroom, Agatha was lying in bed turned the other way. Karen flicked off the light and climbed into bed, hoping for a good night's sleep.

Sleep didn't come quickly and it wasn't solely due to Agatha's snores. She was imagining what her grandmother had looked like, along with her father. In an effort to sleep, she imagined a box and popped all her questions, worries and thoughts about her birth family into the box, closed the lid and handed the box to God. After that, she drifted off to a distant land of wildflower meadows, playful puppies, and early morning sunrises.

CHAPTER 16

THANKS TO AUNT AGATHA'S five o'clock alarm, they were at the train station an hour before the train was due to leave.

When Agatha fell asleep again on the long train ride home, Jason moved to sit next to Karen. "I bet you're excited for when the money's in your bank."

"I am. I'm going to check on Friday. I hope the money would've cleared by then."

"It should be. They said a couple of days, didn't they?"

She nodded.

"It should be well and truly in your account before Friday, then."

"I feel it's all quite unbelievable."

"What's that?"

"To have money. I've been living from payday to payday always watching every dime, and now that burden has been lifted off me."

"*Gott* has blessed you."

"I know." She wondered how Jason made his money. Perhaps he had saved enough money to have a few weeks off while he looked around for work. If he'd been living with his parents for the last few years he would've saved a lot of money not having to pay rent. She wondered if he knew what it was like to live on his own. She swallowed hard and asked him. "Have you ever lived on your own?"

"I moved out of my parents' *haus* when I was nineteen."

"Oh, I didn't know."

"I moved in with two of my close friends. Then they moved out to get married. And now it's just me. I had to move into a smaller place."

"And you still live in a small place now?"

"I do."

"For some reason, I thought you lived at home with your parents."

"Nee, I couldn't wait to get out on my own and be independent."

"Then why is it you don't know how to work a washing machine?"

He chuckled. "I take my washing home to my *mudder,* as you already found out."

"Then, you aren't too independent, are you?"

He shook his head. "I guess not."

~

THEY ARRIVED home on Saturday night and, even though Karen was tired, she forced herself to go to the meeting early the next morning so she could see Jason again.

The meeting was held in Samuel Kauffman's house. When she walked in, she saw Mary and Beth at the back of the room. She made her way through the people standing around talking and sat down beside Mary. Beth was on the other side.

"What happened?" Mary asked.

"I signed the papers and I get the money through to my

bank account this week. And I met my mother." She whispered to the girls and told them what she thought of her mother and the whole experience of traveling with Aunt Agatha. Then they had to stop talking when one of the elders stood to open the meeting in prayer.

When the meeting was finished and everyone gathered outside for the meal afterward, Karen continued talking to her friends while keeping an eye on Jason.

"What happened with you know who?" Mary asked.

"Aunt Agatha?" Karen playfully asked.

"*Nee.* She means Jason," Beth said.

"Ah. Things are going well with him. I really like him a lot. We've arranged to go out again very soon and everything about him suits me." She didn't tell them about his disappointing work ethic because sometimes she felt she was complaining about everything, and she still wasn't sure what to make of it. She didn't want to bring Beth or Mary down. She knew her friends drew happiness from her own.

"You think you'll ever see your mother again? Will she visit you?" Mary asked.

"She took my address and gave me hers." Karen shrugged, still not knowing if she wanted to see her again, or follow up finding out more about her father's side. "Who knows what will happen in the future?"

"That's a good sign that she gave you her address, I guess."

Karen glanced over at Jason and caught his eye, and she couldn't help smiling at him. The other two girls saw who she was looking at.

Beth said, "Go over and speak to him. He's all by himself."

"Okay, I will." She walked over to talk with Jason, hoping he didn't think she was talking about him with her girlfriends.

"Hello, Karen. It's a nice day."

She looked up at the sunny sky. It was midday now and

the sun was directly above them. "It's a lovely day, not too hot and not too cold. What are you doing this week?" she asked him, hoping he would tell her he'd be looking for a job.

"I'm not sure. I'll see what happens. One thing I know, I'll be looking forward to seeing you on Friday."

"Me too. Do you want to meet me for lunch on Friday?"

He frowned. "I'd rather us meet after you finish work."

"I mean, as well as. I'm seeing if the money's in my bank on Friday. I'm going during my lunch break and I don't really want to go by myself." She held her breath and hoped he'd go with her.

His face lit up. "I'd love to accompany you."

A smile spread across her face. "Great. Can you meet me at twelve at the lumberyard?"

"I'll be there."

CHAPTER 17

KAREN SPENT five days dreaming up all the things she could do with the money, and Friday came around fast. At a few minutes to twelve, she packed up her desk and headed to the front of the parking lot of the lumberyard. She'd only just reached the end when he came into view. As always when she saw him, her heart pounded hard.

When he stopped the buggy, she stepped up into it.

"Are you ready?" he asked with a huge grin across his face.

"I am."

He moved the buggy forward. "It's such a big day. *Denke* for sharing it with me. I'm happy you asked me."

"I couldn't think of anyone else I'd rather have come with me." She looked at the road ahead and gave him directions, and teased him again about making sure he knew his left from his right. It was nice to have someone to share things with. She'd felt so alone since her parents had died. First her mother and then her father a year later. Now that all her friends were married, it made them that much more unavailable to do things with.

When they pulled up near the bank, he said, "Shall I wait here?"

"*Nee,* you can come in with me if you'd like."

"Okay."

Once they were in the bank, he stayed at the back of the bank in the small waiting area and she proceeded to the end of the queue. When her turn came, she handed the number of her bank account over the counter. "Could you tell me how much money I have in the bank, please?" She showed her identification card before the teller had a chance to ask.

The woman tapped some keys on the computer. She wrote the amount down on a slip of paper and pushed it forward. "That's your balance."

Karen stared wide-eyed at the amount and was grateful to the grandmother she'd never meet.

"Did you want to take some out now?" the teller asked.

"Not today, thank you. But I'm thinking of buying a house." Those were words she'd never thought she'd say.

The bank teller smiled. "Good idea. Is there anything else I can do for you today?"

Karen shook her head. "Thank you. Goodbye." She turned and immediately saw Jason looking at her. She walked across the lobby to him. "It's there. It's all there."

"Great! Let's celebrate tonight."

"We need to eat now before I go back to work."

They headed out of the bank. "I'm so happy for you, Karen."

"It all seems real now that the money's in my account."

"Now you might shout me a cup of coffee and a sandwich."

"Of course I will."

He laughed. "I was only joking. My treat."

"I'll pay."

"*Nee,* you won't. I will because I'm the man."

She smiled at him. "I don't mind since you're not working."

"I insist."

She couldn't argue with him too much. They found a nearby coffee shop and sat down after ordering.

"How is your life going to change now?" he asked. "Will you still go out with me tonight now that you're so rich?"

"I already said so, so I can't go back on my word." She flashed him a smile.

"You know, that's what I like about you. Well, one of the many things I like about you. You seem like a girl who is never going to change her mind on a whim."

"I don't change my mind often, you're right, but I've never really thought too much about why I'm like that."

"What are you going to buy first?"

"Didn't I tell you?"

"*Nee,* tell me what?" He frowned at her.

"I've been giving it a lot of thought and I would like to buy a *haus.*"

"A *haus?*" He rubbed his chin.

"*Jah.* I was thinking of buying the one I'm living in now."

"But it's small, you said."

"It is, but it suits me just fine." She noticed a significant change on his face. He'd gone from happy to ... to almost sullen. And then the waitress brought the food to their table.

"Ah, so you are going to be a homeowner?" he asked, looking a little brighter.

"I hope so."

"And if Samuel doesn't want to sell it?"

"I'll guess I'll just look around for something else. I'm in no hurry."

They ate their food in silence and when they had finished, Jason drove her back to work.

CHAPTER 18

JUST AS KAREN was about to leave for home, the phone in the office rang. She answered it and heard hysterical crying. "Who is this?"

"Mary," the caller managed to say between sobs.

Karen immediately thought the worse. Damian had hit her. "What's wrong?"

"It's Damian. I have to get away."

Karen spoke over the top of her friend's sobs. "Where are you now?"

"I'm calling from the phone in the barn."

"Where's Damian?"

"I don't know. He walked away in a rage."

Karen guessed she was right that he'd hit her again. "Go to my house. The doors are open. Let yourself in and then lock the doors and windows. If Damian comes there don't open the door and don't let him know you're in there."

"Okay."

"Go now."

She had to cancel her date with Jason. She called his

Uncle Peter's place, but the phone went unanswered. When she called the bishop's house the same thing happened.

When she got home she turned the handle and it was locked. Relieved, she knocked on the door. "Mary, it's me."

She heard the door being unlocked and Mary opened it. She looked dreadful; her eyes were bright red, as was her face.

"Did he hit you?"

"*Nee*, but we just had the worst fight ever."

"Has he hit you before?"

"*Jah*, just the once, but he promised not to do it again."

"You can't go back there, Mary. Stay here tonight."

She picked up a set of keys. "There's a vacant house I can use that's not far from here. Samuel bought it and I was to clean it before his tenants moved in. Can you drive me there?"

"Just stay here."

"I can't. I don't want to get you involved. I'll stay there tonight and then I'll go home and see if he's calmed down. If he knows I've told anyone about our fights, he'll leave me. I'm certain of it."

"I'll just heat up some dinner. And then we'll figure out what to do."

"*Nee*, please drive me now before it gets dark?"

"Okay." She hugged Mary. "Just calm down." She didn't like to see Mary so distressed. "Damian doesn't know about this place?"

"*Nee*." Mary looked downward. "Sometimes we can't make the rent and Samuel lets me clean for him to make up the money. Damian knows I've done work for Samuel in the past, but he doesn't know about this house or where it is."

"Okay. I'll take you there now." Karen hoped she'd be able to change Mary's mind and she'd be able to talk her into seeking help. "I haven't unhitched the buggy, so we can go right now."

Mary stood. "I'm ready."

"Is there furniture?"

"*Nee.*"

"You wait in the buggy. I'll gather some food and pillows and blankets."

Mary sobbed. "*Denke*, Karen."

"I'll be right with you." While Mary went ahead to the buggy, Karen grabbed pen and paper and scribbled a note to Jason. Their date wasn't going to happen. She wrote on the note that she was helping a friend and she'd explain later. Karen slipped the note half under the front doormat, figuring Jason wouldn't miss it. Then she packed a bundle of necessities for Mary's overnight stay.

ON THE DRIVE to the empty house, Mary said, "I don't know what I'm going to do. I wish I'd never married him, but it's too late to change that now."

"Can you both talk to the bishop or somebody? Maybe Hannah?"

"I've asked him to but he wasn't interested. And please don't say anything to anyone or things will just get worse. He keeps saying he'll leave and I'm frightened one day he will. Things are so bad."

"How bad?"

"He's often gone out for most of the night and comes back in the early hours. And he drinks way too much. You're the only person I've told. I can't tell Beth because she'll tell William and then William will want to get involved."

"Yeah, that probably wouldn't be good."

"I don't know what to do."

"You need to tell the bishop. You can't go on being miserable like this."

"He might get worse after talking with the bishop. No one has any idea that anything is wrong with us."

"Well, Beth and I have known it for a while, even before you said anything. You just haven't been yourself."

"All I've ever wanted was a happy marriage and family."

"What did you see in him?"

"I don't know. There was just an immediate attraction. And he was so interested in the Amish, then he converted and went through a lot to do that. He gave up his family, and his friends were all against it. And then he went through the instructions and then the baptism and we waited for six months before we could get married."

It didn't sound like she'd rushed into things. Karen asked, "When did things go bad?"

"Really quickly after we got married."

"Why? Did something happen?"

"It must have, but I can't think what. I think something just changed within him. Maybe he wants to leave me and leave the Amish altogether. I don't know what's going on and I don't know what I can do about it. I'm just miserable all the time."

"Oh, Mary, I'm so sorry."

As soon as Karen settled Mary in the house, she headed back home pleased Mary was safe, for tonight.

CHAPTER 19

JASON PULLED up the buggy outside Karen's house. He'd been a little disappointed when Karen had mentioned buying the small house she was renting. It showed she didn't have her mind fixed on a future with him. Tonight, he hoped he'd get some idea of where things stood between them. He'd wasted too much time on one girl in the past and wasn't going to let that happen a second time.

He jumped down from the buggy and headed over to her front door. Just as he reached the two stone steps leading to the front porch, he saw the note. He headed to it, reached down and picked it up.

The note said she was helping her friend with some kind of emergency and she'd tried calling him. If she'd tried to contact him, maybe that meant she'd wanted his help. He picked up the note, folded it in two and headed back to the buggy while wondering where she could've gone.

Maybe her friend next door might know. He knew Mary lived in the house on the other side of the barn. He left the buggy where it was and walked to the neighboring house. It was only a two-minute walk and when he got there, he knocked on the door. It swung open and Mary's husband stood there staring at him.

"Excuse me for the interruption, but I was wondering if you or your wife might know where Karen is?"

The man's expression didn't change. "Haven't seen her."

"Would your Mary know?" Jason unfolded the paper. "Karen left me this note saying she was helping a friend with some kind of emergency."

"Was she now?"

"Jah."

"Can I see that?" Damian took a step forward.

Jason passed the note over.

When he had read it, Damian passed it back. "It's a fairly sad story."

"What is?"

"No one knows what I'm about to tell you, but since you asked … Mary drinks and sometimes she takes Karen with her. They can be gone all night sometimes." He shook his head and let out a low sigh. "It's awful."

Jason felt the world crashing down around him. *"Nee."*

"Jah, it's true. I'll show you something." Damian took Jason around the side of the house and showed him boxes of empty liquor bottles.

"I can't believe it," Jason said, rubbing his forehead and feeling sick to his stomach.

"Yep. Both of them have gone through these. Karen doesn't want to keep the empties at her house because their third friend, Beth, is over there all the time. That's why Mary won't bring Beth here."

"Karen is a drunkard?" This was the girl he'd imagined a future with. He'd even decided he was going to move to Pleasant Valley for her. "She said she was helping a friend." Was she also a liar?

"Only friend they'd be helping is the man they're buying the drinks from."

Jason stared at Damian. "Why don't you put a stop to your *fraa* doing this?"

Damian shook his head. "I don't know what to do."

"Take it to Bishop Elmer."

He shook his head. "She's threatened me she'll leave me if I ever do that."

"I'm so sorry."

Damian took a step forward and put a hand on Jason's shoulder. "Run a mile. Don't let my problems become yours."

Jason nodded but the stale smell of alcohol coming from Damian, now that he'd moved closer, made Jason doubt his every word. "I appreciate the advice. I had no idea. I was growing fond of Karen."

"You're not from around here, are you?"

"*Nee*, I'm from a different community."

"I'd get as far away from Karen as I could, if I was you. Sometimes, I don't know which one's worse, my wife, or Karen."

"*Denke.* I don't need these problems." Jason left Mary and Damian's house confused. Would the man lie about his own wife and Karen also? If the man was lying, it still didn't answer his question. *Where is Karen?* Could he handle yet another disappointment? His last relationship had been a complete disaster, and had left him hurt, humiliated and embarrassed.

CHAPTER 20

ON SATURDAY, Karen set off walking to the bishop's house as usual, hoping Mary was okay. Just as the house came into view, she saw a taxi turning out of the driveway. It drove in the other direction and she had no idea who was in it. Had Hannah gone into labor?

When she arrived in the house she saw Hannah in the kitchen.

"Morning, Hannah. I thought that might have been you in the taxi going to the hospital."

"*Nee,* it was Jason. He came to say goodbye. Anyway, I'm having the birth at home with Marilyn, our midwife. And, funny you should say that because I have been having slight—."

Karen gasped. "He's gone?"

"Didn't you know?"

Karen pulled out a chair and sat down before she fell down. "Why did he go home so quickly? Was there some kind of emergency?"

"*Nee.* He seemed upset by something. I figured you two

might've disagreed on something or decided you didn't want to progress as a couple."

"*Nee*, we didn't."

"Oh, I'm sorry, Karen. I thought the little trip away would've brought you closer to him."

It was an embarrassing moment. Everybody knew that they liked each other and now it was just plain awkward. Now she agreed with Mary that relationships often weren't easy.

THAT SATURDAY WAS the longest day she'd ever worked at Hannah's house. The chores were dreary and the day dragged on. Maybe Jason didn't believe she had been helping a friend. Is that why he left? The note had been gone, and there had been no wind to blow it away. He must have seen the note.

Just as she was leaving, Hannah told her, "I've been getting small contractions all day."

"The *boppli* will be coming soon?"

"The midwife's on her way. I think he'll be born tonight if it's anything like the last two births."

"You are in pain?"

"*Nee*, not yet. The contractions are pretty regular and they're gradually getting stronger but not painful."

Karen winced. She didn't want to know how painful childbirth was until she was faced with it herself. At that time, she would ask questions; before that she didn't want to know.

"That's exciting. I can't wait to see it. I mean, him or her."

"I'm going to help with the birthing," Rebecca said.

"Really? You think you'll be able to handle it?" Karen asked.

"Jah, I was at the last two of *Mamm's* births. I want to become a midwife when I grow up."

Her mother overheard. "You're too forgetful for that. You'd forget how far along the women were or you'd forget to check on them when they were in labor."

"Mamm, that's not nice."

Hannah chuckled.

"Do you need me to do anything, Hannah?" Karen asked.

"Nee denke. You go home and pray for me."

"I will. I'll pray all goes well."

$$\sim$$

THE NEXT DAY, Karen was relieved to see her two friends. Both Beth and Mary were there. Mary brought back the bundle of pillows and blankets and told Karen that Damian had calmed down by the time she'd walked back home. He'd fallen asleep and didn't even know she'd slept elsewhere that night. They'd all heard the news that Bishop Elmer and Hannah had been blessed with another boy.

Karen had decided she would wait until Saturday to visit, knowing they'd have way too many well-wishers stopping by.

THE WHOLE WEEK went by with Karen upset that Jason had left so suddenly and without a word. They'd grown so close in such a short time and she'd dreamed of a future with him.

When Saturday came, Karen arrived extra early so she could take a look at the new baby.

She opened the door and found Rebecca sitting on the couch. "Oh, it's you. He's back."

"Who's back?"

"You know."

"Jason?"

"That's right. He's back. He's come to see the *boppli*. Anyway, that's what he said. But he didn't bother coming to see the last three. I reckon he's only come back to see you. To say sorry for what he did."

She frowned at Rebecca. "He didn't *do* anything."

"Why did he just up and leave? He must've done something. Or was it you?"

"It's complicated." She couldn't tell him about Mary and the reason she'd had to miss their date. "It's complicated, just like you and Dean."

Rebecca jumped to her feet. "There's nothing going on with me and Dean."

"Really? You're getting very upset by just the mention of his name."

Rebecca frowned. "It's awful. People think we'll marry and have thought that since we were ten years old."

Karen put a hand lightly on her shoulder. "I'm only teasing. I've heard that too, but don't let it get to you. How's the new *boppli?*"

A smile spread across Rebecca's face. "He's too cute and so tiny."

"Can I see him?"

"Later. *Mamm* and *Dat* are still asleep. He was crying all night."

It was odd that the bishop was still asleep. He was normally such an early riser. "I guess I'll have to wait. I'll start on the laundry."

IT WAS MIDMORNING when Jason came to the house. He walked up to Karen as she pinned out the clean wet clothes. "Hi, Karen."

She spun around to face him.

CHAPTER 21

"I was hoping to see you," Karen said to Jason.

"Were you?" He took off his hat.

"Jah, I was." She pinned out the last shirt and then had to tell him the truth of how she felt. "I was upset you left so suddenly."

"You weren't there when I went to see you."

"I left a note. Didn't you get it?"

He nodded.

"I had a good reason for not going on our date." She picked up the empty laundry basket.

"That's what I realized. I was angry when you weren't there and sometimes I act too hastily. That was one of those times. I came back here to ask your forgiveness for leaving with no word."

"You're forgiven. The thing is, I left because a friend was in great need."

He fiddled nervously with his hat, turning it in a circular motion. "What friend?"

She shook her head. "I can't tell you. Sorry. It's something that she wants to keep secret."

"You can't tell me?"

"Nee, I can't and I'm truly sorry."

He huffed. "Then that tells me that this whole thing was a mistake."

"You mean you and I are a mistake, do you?"

JASON PLACED his hat firmly on his head. "It was silly of me to think that anything could come of it."

"I don't understand. Why is that silly?"

"You weren't born into the community."

"You're right. Perhaps we're just too different. We think very differently about things."

His jaw dropped open. He was goading her, teasing, and she didn't bite back. Immediately, he was ashamed of himself. "Are you serious?"

"Well, isn't that what you think?"

He shook his head. "You're so quick to throw things away."

"But you just said … What am I throwing away?"

"The chances of us making something together. Having some kind of a future together. Don't you want that?"

Karen looked down at the ground. "I admit I did at one point."

He inched closer to her. "Then tell me what changed?"

She looked up at him. "You did."

"Perhaps you changed, Karen. You got this money and all of a sudden you don't need …"

"What? What don't I need, Jason?"

"You don't need a man to lean on."

"It's not like that. Not really."

He wanted to know how she was feeling, but she wasn't letting him in. "You're not making a lot of sense and I'm probably not either. How about we try again? Will you give us another chance?" He smiled at her.

"Will you give me one?" she asked.

Then he knew things would be okay. "I will. *Jah,* I will."

"Very good. That's all I wanted to hear."

Rebecca came rushing out of the back door. "Jason and Karen, do you want to see the *boppli* now?"

They both stared at her.

"Come in and see him. *Mamm* is asking where you both are; she saw you arrive, Jason."

"We'd love to," Jason said.

THEY BOTH WALKED into Hannah's room to see the sleeping baby. Hannah was sitting up in bed.

"Oh, he's so beautiful," Karen said.

"And another boy," Jason added. "What a surprise."

"We would've been surprised by a girl," Hannah said with amusement.

"He's lovely, Aunt Hannah. Now, I'll head off. I just wanted to see the new addition and I approve," Jason said and then he left the room while Hannah and Karen laughed quietly.

"What are you calling him?" Karen asked as she stood leaning over the baby and marveling at his small and perfect features.

"We've got a few ideas, but we haven't made up our minds just yet. Do you have any thoughts?"

Rebecca said, "There's probably no names left. You've used them all, *Mamm.*"

"Stop it, Rebecca," Hannah said with a smile.

Karen took her eyes off the baby for a moment. "I like the name Andrew."

"That's a nice name," Hannah said, looking across at the baby. *"Jah,* it's a strong name and it's one we haven't used before. I'll add that to the list and Elmer and I will talk about it tonight."

"And how are you feeling, Hannah?" Karen asked as she and Rebecca sat on the end of the bed.

"Good, but I'm still going to enjoy a few days in bed before I have to get back into the normal household duties. I hope he doesn't take too much longer to sort out his days and nights."

"Everything is under control, *Mamm.* Stay in bed as long as you need."

Hannah smiled. "I'll stay for a while, but I'm not one for resting too much."

"You should enjoy the rest while you can," Karen said.

"I'm doing okay."

Karen peered over at the baby once more. "How long will he sleep for?"

"I have just fed him, so he might sleep for a couple more hours at least."

"What color eyes does he have?"

Hannah answered, "They're dark blue, but I'm guessing they'll go brown like the rest of them. They take after me. Elmer's the only one of us with blue eyes."

"And what do the others think of him?" Karen asked.

"They're interested. Even the *boppli.*"

"He's not the *boppli* anymore," Rebecca said.

"Nee, he's not. We'll have to start calling him Joel now, won't we?"

"Jah."

Karen stood up. "Let me know if you need any extra help. I can come before and after work."

"We'll be fine. Your Saturdays are a big help."

"Well, just let me know. Call me at work if I'm needed."

"Denke, but I have plenty of helpers."

Karen left them and walked downstairs. Jason was in the living room speaking with the bishop. They stood up when she approached.

"Your *boppli* is just beautiful," she said to the bishop.

"He is lovely. *Gott* has blessed us many times."

"He has."

"Can I drive you home, Karen?" Jason asked. "I've borrowed Peter's buggy and it's outside."

"That's okay. I'll walk and I don't finish here until four." When Karen walked back into the kitchen, Jason followed.

Karen spun around, and said, "About the other day, I can understand how you would've felt. I had no way of contacting you. I called your *Onkel* Peter's place and no one answered. I had no other way of getting a message to you. I even tried calling here to leave a message and no one answered here either."

"How about we put us that behind us and never mention it again? We've talked about it enough."

"Done."

He smiled at her. "I shouldn't have been upset. Something always goes wrong when I plan a date with you for Friday nights. How about we do something during the day Sunday instead?"

Sunday afternoon was when she saw her friends and she couldn't change that now, not when Mary was having so many problems with Damian. "I already have something arranged for Sunday. And it's not something I can get out of."

"What about Sunday night?" he asked without hesitation.

"That would be perfect. You're staying the week?"

"*Jah.* I'll see you then if I don't see you before. I can come back and drive you home today."

"*Nee, denke.* I'll enjoy the walk and it'll be a chance to clear my head. I've had an eventful couple of weeks."

He nodded. "Okay."

AFTER SHE FINISHED WORK, she walked home feeling pleased to be back on track with Jason, but she couldn't live her life around a man. One thing she wanted and one thing that would give her security was her own home. She didn't want her moods to be dependent on a man. She wanted to create a good life for herself with or without Jason. The house she lived in was small but if she married Jason, they could build onto it. Even though she didn't know his exact financial situation, she doubted he'd ever have money to buy them a home. He'd feel better about not being able to provide them a home if she already had one.

WHEN SHE GOT BACK to her house, she immediately hitched the buggy and headed to her landlord's house, hoping he'd be home.

CHAPTER 22

AFTER KAREN SECURED HER BUGGY, she approached Samuel Kauffman's large house with nerves gnawing at her tummy. She had no idea how much her *haus* was worth. She stepped up to the front door and knocked.

A minute later, his housekeeper Freda opened the door. "Karen, hello."

"Hello. Would I be able to speak with Samuel?"

Freda fully opened the door. "*Jah*, come in."

"*Denke.*"

"Stay there," Freda said, as soon as she was inside the modest entry area. "I'll tell him you're here."

Samuel walked out after a few minutes. "Karen. Is everything all right at the *haus?*"

"*Jah*, it is. I was wondering if you'd sell it." Nerves had made her blurt out her query.

He crossed his arms over his chest. "Who wants to know?"

"Me. I came into an inheritance."

"Oh, I'm happy for you, but the *haus* isn't for sale. What made you think it was?" He narrowed his hazel eyes.

"I know it's not, but I thought perhaps you could sell it to me and buy something else."

He shrugged his shoulders. "Why would I do that?"

She could feel her cheeks redden. He was handsome, but that wasn't what had made him intimidating. It was his manner. He had an air of superiority about him that none of the other Amish men had. He was nothing like his sister, Beth. "No reason. I thought there was no harm in asking. I'm sorry to waste your time. Goodbye, Samuel." She turned to leave.

"Wait a moment."

She swung back around.

He cleared his throat. "Are you certain you'd want to buy it? Wouldn't you prefer something else? Have you looked around?"

"*Nee*, I haven't. The place just suits me and I like living there."

"Hmm. You see, the difficulty for me is that the barn serves your place and the one next door."

"Oh, so the barn belongs to the *haus* I'm in, and not Mary and Damian's?"

"*Jah*, so if you buy that one, that leaves me overcharging Mary and Damian and they'll lose their barn space and … Leave it with me, I'll think on it."

"You will?"

"I'm not promising anything. How much were you thinking it's worth?"

Her eyes widened. She was hoping he'd name a price. "I don't know what the value is."

He scoffed. "Surely you've got some idea."

"*Nee*, I don't. But your property-tax papers should have a baseline value listed."

"I'll have my realtor make an estimate. Then, we'll see

what arrangement we can come to. That is, if you've got your heart set on it."

She nodded furiously. "I do. I really do."

"Okay, I'll set the wheels in motion."

"Really?"

"Jah. Don't get too excited, though.

"Denke, denke so much. I can hardly believe it."

"Don't let anyone know I'm thinking of this."

She laughed. "You don't want to ruin your reputation?"

"Exactly. I don't want to lose all my investments. What would happen if I sold all my houses to my tenants?"

She wanted to wrap her arms around him and then thought better of it. *He'd be sure I was crazy!* He hadn't said he'd sell, but she could see he was getting used to the idea. *"Denke,* Samuel."

"I'll be in touch." He walked to the front door and opened it for her.

CHAPTER 23

THAT NIGHT, Jason figured he would ask his Uncle Peter's advice about women—one woman in particular.

"You were being very quiet over dinner Jason, and not like your usual self."

The children had gone to bed and his Aunt Barbara was busy in the kitchen. "Well, you know how *Onkel* Elmer asked me to go away to help ..."

"I know, to help Karen."

"That's right. Anyway, Karen ... I might like her." He laughed at how his words stuck in his mouth.

"What do you think is funny? What is troubling you so much about her?"

"That's the thing. It was going brilliantly and then she pulled back. I'm pretty sure she liked me and then now I feel that perhaps she doesn't and I was mistaken." It weighed on his mind that she hadn't wanted him to drive her home. If she really liked him, wouldn't she have wanted him to drive her home?

"Have you talked to her about it?"

"*Nee,* I couldn't. We don't say things like that to one another."

"Well, she might be thinking about you too," Peter said.

"You think so?"

Peter's face softened. "I'm older; I know these things."

"I thought you might. Has she been involved with anybody else in the community that you know of?"

His uncle straightened up and scratched his head. "I can't say it because I don't remember. Nothing serious anyway, not to my knowledge." Peter leaned forward. "You want me to find out? Barbara knows everything that's going on."

Jason shook his head. "If you ask any questions, everyone will know you're asking for me and I'll feel a fool."

"You might look like a fool, but I won't ask any questions."

"Good." Jason didn't know if his uncle was trying to be funny or not.

"Does she know you like her?"

Jason nodded. "I'm fairly certain. *Jah,* she must from what we've both said to one another."

"How about you make a grand gesture? *Maidels* like things like that, and make it a romantic one."

"Take her flowers?"

Peter curled his lip. "Something like that but bigger. Give it some thought."

"*Jah,* I should give it some thought, and I will."

~

When Karen was getting ready for her date with Jason, she heard the phone in the barn. She'd never make it in time to answer it, but still, she made a dash for it. When the ringing stopped, she kept going hoping they'd call back. It rang again and Karen managed to answer it before it stopped. "Hello."

"Karen, it's me."

It was Jason and she knew from the sound of his voice they wouldn't be meeting that night. "Is something wrong?"

"Peter's horse is lame."

"Oh, that's disappointing, but it's okay. I'll see you during the week sometime, then."

"I'm sorry, Karen. I was looking forward to this. How about we make it Monday for dinner instead? I'll collect you at your place before it gets dark."

"That'll be fine." Karen knew he was cooling off. He hadn't suggested she collect him, and besides that, he could've walked the short distance to Elmer's house and borrowed one of his buggies. "I'll see you later."

"Bye, Karen."

She hung up the phone's receiver and hurried back to the house not wanting to bump into Damian. That was the only drawback of the house—the shared barn. At least the barn was divided into two sections with separate entrances, the only common area being the space where the phone was located.

With her disappointing love life, it was now more important than ever that she have her own house for security.

~

WHEN KAREN GOT to work the next day, she found a note on her desk. She scanned to the bottom and saw it was from Samuel Kauffman. The note read, *Please meet me at my house after you finish work. We can discuss your house.*

That was good news. Now that she had the money, she wanted to do something wise with it and what better thing could she do than buy the house that she loved?

LATER THAT AFTERNOON, Karen knocked on Samuel's door and this time he opened it, rather than Freda, his housekeeper.

"Come in."

She followed him through a long hallway until he opened the door to a combination study and office.

"Have a seat," he said, pointing to a chair. She obeyed and before she could say anything, he said, "I need to tell you something before we discuss the price. I have another buyer who is interested in the *haus.*"

Her heart sank. This wasn't good, but in a way, she was used to this kind of thing. It was just like dreaming of marrying Jason and then feeling him slipping away. "We had a deal."

"We most definitely did not. I told you I'd consider it. I said there was the issue with the shared barn."

"I was thinking about that. With the money you get from my *haus* you could build them a barn. This one's not that close to their *haus.*"

He shook his head. "I've thought about that. It's not an ideal solution because their rent is adjusted accordingly for their barn being shared, and so far from the house."

"Oh."

"We could possibly still have a deal, but I'm a businessman and I need to listen to this other offer."

She blew out a deep breath. "And how much is this person offering?" Whatever it was she'd offer him more. She was sure the place wasn't worth anything remotely close to three hundred. Yet, he still hadn't named a figure. "What did the realtor say about the value?"

"The realtor gave me an estimate without looking through the house, but I've told the other buyer he can have a look through it this afternoon at five."

Her mouth fell open in shock. It was after four already. "Aren't you required to give me more notice than that?"

"Technically, I suppose I am, but aren't you in a hurry to buy this place?"

"I'm not in an actual hurry, as long as I know that I can buy it. I don't want anybody else to buy it out from under me."

He interlocked his fingers and stared at her. "I have already given my word that he could have a look through the house at five. It will only take a few minutes, and then we'll talk further and I'll consider your offer and his offer, if he makes one."

"You haven't told me how much yet."

"I'm biding my time."

She stared at him, not knowing what that meant. The whole thing was becoming too hard. "Why would you even entertain selling it to somebody else? It doesn't make sense. You can only sell it once."

"I was not considering selling it at all until you raised the question."

She had nothing to say.

"This is how business works. You don't expect me to give the place away to you, do you?"

"Of course not. I told you I came into an inheritance. I can pay a good price for it. A fair price for both of us. I didn't think you'd be shopping the property around."

He shrugged his shoulders. "Business is business. How about this, if this man doesn't buy the *haus*, I'll give you the option to buy it."

"'If' he doesn't buy it? If he gives you an offer, will you give me a chance to make a higher one?"

"Of course."

She put a hand on her chest and breathed out. "Good."

"We'll talk further about this tomorrow. I'll stop by the lumberyard tomorrow morning, okay?"

"Okay, *denke.*"

SHE LEFT Samuel's house feeling defeated. If the whole thing was so hard, maybe she wasn't meant to buy the place. Her mother's words came to mind then, *"Gott* makes a way where there is no way." She had to hold on to hope.

When she got into the buggy her first thought was to tidy up the house for the person coming to look at it. But, she thought, why would she make the place look better for this person to buy the house from under her? She reminded herself then that making the place look better was the right thing to do. As much as she didn't like Samuel going back on his word, he was the owner and as the tenant she should do her duty. She'd always kept the place clean, but it wasn't as tidy as it could be at the moment.

When she got home, she hurried around tidying. There were fabric pieces and bits and pieces from craft projects lying around. Then, when she was satisfied the place looked good, she paced up and down waiting for the person. A few minutes before five, Jason arrived and she immediately remembered their date. Why did something always go wrong when they planned a date? It seemed things were always blocking her when she wanted something.

She hurried out to the buggy. "Jason, I'm so sorry I forgot you were meeting me here. Can you come back in half an hour?"

He got down from the buggy. "Why's that?"

She nibbled on a fingernail and didn't want to tell him. She didn't want to be the kind of woman who complained non-stop. "Oh, it's so terrible. Samuel said that he's got someone else who wants to buy the house now. I'm supposed to show them through this afternoon."

"What's so terrible about that?

"Because I wanted to buy it."

Jason laughed, and she frowned at him.

"Why is this so funny? It is absolutely the most frustrating thing I can think of."

"I'm the other buyer, Karen."

She stared at him. "You? What could you possibly want with my *haus?*"

"I want it for us to move into after we get married."

Her hand flew to her mouth. "Married?"

He nodded and stepped closer. "It's not about this place. You can buy it, or I'll buy it, but the one thing I do want is for us to be married. I don't care where we live."

She'd always thought he was a penniless drifter. "You have the money to buy this place?"

"I'd like to say yes. I don't have the entire amount. I would have to take out a small loan, but your friend and landlord, Samuel Kauffman, gave me a figure of what it was worth and I'm twenty thousand shy of that mark."

"Really?" That was a huge shock. It wasn't that she wanted a man with money, she wanted a man with drive, determination and a good work ethic.

"He said I could pay the rest off to him."

"He said that?"

"He's a businessman. And, apparently a moneylender."

Everything was falling into place, but still, she was scared. Damian had seemed lovely to everyone including Mary. What if Jason turned out to be like Damian? There could be nothing worse for a woman. Bishop Elmer had always said a wife is to be cherished, and Karen wanted a man who would do exactly that.

"What do you say?" he said, staring at her with his clear blue eyes.

She had to be truthful. "I'm scared."

"Of me?"

"Of the whole idea of marriage."

"I see. You never intend to marry?"

"I want to."

CHAPTER 24

JASON STARED AT KAREN, not knowing what to do. Maybe she did want to get married, but not to him. That certainly wasn't the signals he thought she'd been sending. He was sure she liked him most of the time, but the more he thought about it, the more he realized her signals had been mixed. She clearly didn't know her own mind. He couldn't get involved with another woman like that.

This was a grand gesture like his uncle had suggested. He didn't know what more he could do to show how he felt about her.

He had been sure this would've gone in a whole different direction. She would giggle about him being the other buyer and would fall into his arms professing undying love and devotion. Then with light and love in her eyes she would turn her face upward and he would lower his head until his lips met hers for their very first kiss. Then, they'd go out for dinner and talk about their wedding and set a definite date. Naturally, they would live in the house and he'd buy it from Samuel and he'd feel like a proper provider for his new wife.

Instead he just stood there feeling like a fool. This was the last time he'd take advice from his uncle.

Were things ruined between them? Would they still go on their date tonight? Things were certainly awkward. As he always did when he was nervous, he took his hat off and ran a hand through his hair. "Um, do you want to think about it?"

"Can I?"

It wasn't ideal and made him feel that she didn't want him. "Of course you can. It's a big decision." What would he say to Samuel? He'd have to give him an answer on the house. Their deal was practically done, aside from signing papers and paying the deposit. He'd already arranged to meet him mid-morning of the next day to do just that. "Do you still want to go out tonight?"

"Do you mind if we make it tomorrow instead?"

"Sure, that's okay, but you don't have to go out with me at all just to be polite."

"Oh, it's not that. I want to, but … I am feeling a bit over-whelmed tonight. I got a little rattled when Samuel told me he had another buyer when he'd already as good as promised the place to me."

"Then I further put pressure on you by proposing. I'm sorry."

"*Nee, nee.* Don't say sorry. I will definitely give it some serious thought. Is that okay?"

"*Jah.*" He hoped he hadn't ruined everything. Maybe he'd taken things too quickly without waiting for a green light. "I'm sorry if I gave you a fright. About the house, I mean, and about my ill-time proposal."

"*Nee,* it's not about you. You've done nothing wrong. These problems are all mine. All in my head, I think. I just need to sort things out."

"There's no pressure. Take as long as you want. Take years if you need. But don't be afraid to tell me you won't accept my proposal. You won't upset me, I mean, I will be disappointed of course, but you must make the decision for yourself not taking anything else into account."

"Denke."

He smiled at her and noticed she did nothing to reassure him. If only she had. He felt almost like he'd been slapped in the face. "Good night, Karen." He turned to take up the reins of his buggy.

"Good night."

He got back into his buggy and drove away. He didn't look back at her and neither did he wave. The whole thing had turned out a horrendous mess.

KAREN STARED at Jason leaving in the buggy and was just about to wave when she noticed he didn't look back. He was upset, she could see that. She was in love with him. She'd never felt like this about anyone, but every time she wanted to give her heart and her mind to Jason, the stories Mary had told about Damian and her marriage jumped into her mind.

She had some serious thinking to do and needed some motherly advice. Normally, she would've talked to Hannah, but she'd be too busy with the new baby. There was Beth, but over the last two years she'd been depressed due to her childless state and Karen didn't want to add to her depression. The next person who came to mind was old Aunt Agatha. Seeing it was still early, Karen decided to stop by her house.

≈

SHE KNOCKED on Agatha's door hoping the old lady wouldn't mind a visitor.

"Good girl, that's a good girl," she heard Agatha say on the other side of the door. "We have someone at the door."

Agatha opened the door and then Karen noticed two large tabby cats purring around Agatha's feet. "This is a nice surprise."

"I hope you don't mind me visiting. I needed advice, and I didn't know who else to turn to."

Aunt Agatha's lips curved upward into a huge grin. "I'm glad you came to me. Advice is something I'm not short on. Come inside. We'll sit by the fire."

It wasn't cold enough for a fire, so Karen sat in the furthest chair.

"Well, go ahead, dear."

"Okay, so there is a person I like." She jumped a little when a cat sprang at her.

"It's only Tabby. He won't bite you unless you move."

The tiger-like cat was large, larger than any cat she'd ever seen. "Hello, Tabby." He half closed his eyes and then proceeded to make himself comfortable in her lap. The other cat sat down next to Agatha, staring at Karen.

"You can pat him, but that's all," Agatha cautioned.

She patted the cat. "How do you know when you're a match with someone?"

"If you're matched with someone, you don't need to ask those questions."

"I see, and normally I wouldn't, but I have this friend who married someone and she was sure she was in love with him and now they have the most miserable life." Karen made sure she stayed still as she talked.

Agatha leaned forward. "Who is this couple?"

"I can't say."

Agatha straightened up. "Quite right. That's right that you don't tell me who they are. But if you did tell me I would keep it in the strictest of confidence."

"I can't even if you never tell another person, I just can't."

Agatha's mouth turned down at the corners. "What are you telling me about this other person for?"

"My point is, this other person was in love with this man and then he turned horrible and now they both have a miserable life together. I don't want that to happen to me. How do I know if this person I like will change after we marry or not?"

"You have to have faith."

She considered what Agatha said for a moment. "But my friend had faith."

"I haven't seen anyone who's had a bad marriage in our community. Maybe there were one or two over the years who didn't get along too well, but all of those marriages had been hasty."

"Is the secret not to have a hasty marriage?"

"I don't know. I married my Hezekiah when we were both seventeen, a month after we met, and we were very happy together. There is no secret formula for love or whether a marriage is going to be happy or sad."

Karen huffed and kept petting the cat. "It's just such a commitment. I mean, how do you really know a person? I suppose you never really do know another person deep down and yet..."

"Do we really know ourselves?"

She stared helplessly at Aunt Agatha. She came to get answers not more questions.

"Has he asked you to marry him?" Agatha asked.

"Um.... *jah,* just now."

Agatha clapped her hands together with delight. "What did you say?"

"I'm thinking about it. That's why I've come to you for advice. I've only got my friends and I thought someone more experienced would be better, so I decided I'd ask you."

Agatha sat staring at her with a troubled face replacing the delighted one of seconds before.

Karen continued, "Is there any advice you can give me? Any at all?" Someone as old as she was must have some advice to share.

"I've been giving you advice." Aunt Agatha leaned forward and pulled out her ears. "You must use these to hear what I'm saying."

Karen sat silently.

"I feel sorry for your friend, whose name you're keeping quiet. You see, she must realize she didn't marry the wrong one. Marriage is a commitment we make, and there can be no ridiculous questions after we marry whether we've made the right choice. We don't build a house on shifting sand and neither do we build a marriage on a shifting sandy foundation. We build the marriage on the rock, which is the word of *Gott*."

"That sounds good in theory, but where does love fit in?" Karen wondered if love could overcome all problems. Did she love Jason enough to marry him if she had all these doubts?

"Love is a choice. His word is clear. Mark 10:9 *What therefore God hath joined together, let not man put asunder.*"

"But what if she—my friend is willing to do all that, but her husband isn't?" Karen was asking about her friend, but applying the answer to a situation she too might face in the future.

"Then she must be steadfast, strong, and pray he sees the light. She can be a loving Godly example to him. At some point, the man will realize he's not in right standing with *Gott* and will find his way back to the narrow path."

"It all sounds good in theory,"

Agatha heaved a sigh, and the cat next to her moved to lie down. "Perhaps you're looking at your friend's life too much

128

rather than concentrating on your own? Have you ever thought she's being a negative influence on you if she's giving you all these doubts? Proverbs 12:26 *The righteous is more excellent than his neighbour: but the way of the wicked seduceth them.* Proverbs 13:20 *He that walketh with wise men shall be wise: but a companion of fools shall be destroyed."*

"She's a lovely person and the nicest person you'd ever meet. She's just having a hard time of it."

"She'd do well to read more of the bible. I do love the Proverbs. Chapter 17 and verse 3. *The fining pot is for silver, and the furnace for gold: but the Lord trieth the hearts."*

Karen nodded, realizing that the scriptures were Agatha's answer to everything, but some things needed some kind of practical application for the modern day. If the scriptures held all the answers, what happened when someone didn't take heed of them? It didn't seem fair that Mary was stuck with Damian who abused her and pretended to all he was Godly. Then and there, Karen decided she'd have another talk with Mary about having a word with Bishop Elmer. Mary couldn't continue this way. Perhaps all Damian needed was a good talk with the bishop. And, if that drove Damian to leave rather than change his ways, might Mary be better off alone instead of living in fear?

"Continue slowly and prayerfully is the only advice I can give you. Also, take a good long look at the man's friends and family. Does he come from a good family?"

"I can't say."

"It always helps to know their friends. You know what the Bible says about family and friends, *jah?"*

"What does it say? I know. Um, it says something in Proverbs about a man … you can judge a man by his friends? Something like that?" Karen gulped and then shifted the focus off her substandard knowledge of the verse in question. "It's amazing how you can say those scriptures off the top of your head."

"I was raised having to recite them at night. You young people today need time to read the Bible. It really does answer your questions."

"I will learn them better. The scriptures are such a comfort."

"The bible is *Gott's* guidebook for our life; it contains answers for every question we could ever ask."

Karen nodded. "I'll keep that in mind." When the cat started purring and digging its claws into her leg, she said, "It's late. I should go."

"Thank you for visiting me. Would you like to sample some of my baking before you go?"

The old lady looked so excited that Karen said, *"Jah,* that would be nice."

"I made gramma pie this morning," Agatha said as her face lit up.

If there was one thing Karen couldn't stand it was gramma pie, a rich, milk-and-eggs custard pie spiced with nutmeg, but she just couldn't disappoint Aunt Agatha. "Lovely. I would love to try some."

"Come with me to the kitchen."

"Um, what do I do with the cat?" Karen stared at the cat in her lap. It was growing heavier by the minute.

Agatha leaned over and carefully lifted the cat and placed her on the couch. "There's a *gut* girl."

As Agatha and Karen ate pie, Karen heard more about Agatha's views on marriage.

That led Karen to wonder, what advice would her parents, the ones who had raised her, have given?

CHAPTER 25

JASON PULLED up at Samuel's house and a young Amish boy from the community ran up to him to secure his horse.

"Denke. I have an appointment with Samuel."

"He's home," the young boy said.

Jason walked up to the house. This appointment was to secure the deal for the house. He felt more of a fool having to tell a successful and accomplished man like Samuel that he'd been rejected and fallen flat on his face in regard to his marriage proposal. But still, he had no other choice. He had to go ahead with the meeting to tell Samuel it hadn't worked out and he couldn't buy the property now.

He blew out a deep breath as he stood before the door and, before he was ready to knock, the door opened and Samuel stood there. "How did the proposal work out?"

Jason shook his head.

Samuel tilted his head. "She said no?"

"Not exactly."

"Come inside." He was quickly ushered through to Samuel's office and he sat down. Once they were both seated Samuel said, "I take it you're not buying the *haus* now?"

"I'm sorry. I feel like such an idiot. I was sure she'd say yes and be thrilled about me buying the *haus* for her — for us."

"She flatly refused you?"

Jason gave a little shrug. *"Nee.* She said she'd think about it." He could see that Samuel felt sorry for him. "I'm sorry to muck you about like this."

"Women! You never know what they're thinking. I'm used to dealing with men. Men are logical and business is logical; it's all just numbers. But women ..." He shook his head. "I've never been able to work them out."

Jason laughed and didn't feel quite so bad, knowing other men had experienced things like that. "You ever come close to being married?"

"I've had a few women I thought I might marry, but I was taking my time and in each case, the woman in question got sick of waiting."

"How long did you make them wait?"

"Two years once, another one eighteen months, and one of them a year."

"And you weren't sure about them?"

"I guess I wasn't and maybe that's why I was hesitating."

"I'm sure about Karen," Jason said.

"Jah, she's one of my *schweschder's* close friends and Beth doesn't make friends easily. That says a lot about Karen."

Jason leaned forward. "You've got two of your *schweschder's* friends renting two of your properties?"

He chuckled. "I have quite a few residences I lease in Pleasant Valley."

"And you have a few businesses too, I hear."

"That's right."

"Well, if she eventually accepts my proposal I might come knocking on your door looking for a job."

Samuel shook his head. "What you should be doing is

working for yourself. The best thing I ever did was start my own business instead of working for a paycheck."

"I'm working out what to do with myself. I used to do a lot of construction, but I've hurt my back. I bought a bakery back home; the owner was selling because it wasn't doing so well. I changed things around and the old staff left. With the new equipment, some new offerings, and new staff, it's doing better than I ever could've hoped. That allowed me the freedom to come here for a few weeks."

"You must have good staff."

"I do."

Samuel slapped his hand down on the desk. "I knew it! You're a businessman, just like me."

Jason chuckled. "I might be like you in a much smaller way. All I have is the bakery."

"Maybe you could open one close by and replicate the one you already have. If you're not buying the *haus*, put the money into the business."

"That's a good idea, but if Karen doesn't accept my proposal there'll be nothing to keep me here."

Samuel pressed his lips together and slowly nodded. "If I can be of any help with anything let me know."

"*Denke.* I appreciate your understanding, and your insights." Jason stood, leaned over the desk and extended his hand and Samuel stood and shook it.

JASON LEFT Samuel's house feeling better. He deliberately hadn't told Karen he had a bakery, because he didn't even want to think about the manager, Leah. Things had been going brilliantly between him and Leah, he thought, and then she suddenly told him things were over. And the next week she was openly dating David Bontrager. She was a very good bakery manager, and their work relationship was still fine.

He'd gone to Pleasant Valley in the hopes of mending his broken heart. He hadn't gone there intending to fall in love again. His feelings for Leah, he now realized, had never been as intense as his feelings for Karen.

～

KAREN WONDERED how long Jason would give her to consider his proposal. She'd already pushed him away, she felt, by not accepting his proposal immediately.

When she got home from Aunt Agatha's, she sat down and opened her grandmother's letter and read through it twice. It felt nice that someone had been thinking about her all these years. Was she feeling so scared of getting close to someone because she'd been adopted out and not wanted by her birth mother?

Fearing Jason might come to the house for her answer, she grabbed her black coat and headed out the door. She'd go for a walk by the river. The river always helped her to think. Maybe it had something to do with the running water or being close to nature. Whatever it was, she wanted to be alone. She slipped into the coat and buttoned it up.

Just as she started out the rain fell gently. It wasn't enough to even get wet, just enough to make the surroundings fresher. Although it was dark, she knew the clouds were blowing away and the darkness of the night sky would shortly be lit by the full moon.

There was no one else she could ask advice from. The only thing she could do was something she should've done in the first place, and that was talk to God. He had all the answers.

CHAPTER 26

KAREN WALKED through the paddocks that separated her house from the river. Just as she reached the dense line of trees along the riverbank, an owl hooted, swooping low over her head and scaring her half to death. She looked to see where it had gone and saw it disappearing into the high branches of a tall tree. Tugging her coat further around her body and taking a slow deep breath to calm her racing heart, she continued. Then she stepped onto the narrow path that led to the riverbank.

Peace washed over her when the gentle babble of the water met her ears. When the river came into view, she watched in wonder as the moonbeams danced on the water creating a sparkling wonderland.

As she listened to the gentle lapping of the water, she knew she had to pray out loud. This place was as serene and tranquil as though it was at heaven's door. She could feel God's presence here and was sure He was listening.

Her thoughts went to Jason. If she married him she knew there would be no turning back, no chance to marry a second time to get it right. She couldn't just marry him because it was convenient like Aunt Agatha advised. Even if he was her last hope for a husband, being alone was a far better choice than being in a bad marriage. But, if she said no, what if she was missing a wonderful man, a happy marriage, and a good life?

"Dear *Gott*, I come before you and I need the right answer. I need to know what to do. Jason seems so wonderful, but I've seen what a bad marriage can be like. I know it can happen in the community. Just because we all try to walk the narrow way doesn't mean we're all going to stay on it. And if someone falls off, I don't want to be dragged with them. I know life doesn't come with guarantees of fairness or freedom from tragedy, but one thing I've always wanted is a happy family. I don't want to marry Jason if he's going to turn out like Damian." Her heart froze when she heard rustling in the bushes. It sounded like an animal—a large one.

"Did you say, 'Turn out like Damian'?"

It was a man. She swung around. It was worse than a wild animal. It was Damian, and he'd clearly heard every private word she'd uttered to God. Then the dark figure walked closer and she moved away from the riverbank, fearing he might push her in. She couldn't swim and with her thick coat and heavy shoes, she'd surely sink to the bottom.

When he got closer, her gaze dropped to the bottle in his hand and from the way he was staggering she knew he'd been drinking awhile. It seemed she'd happened across his private drinking spot. "You heard me?"

"Yes, I heard you and your pious little prayer. All of you make me sick and I don't know what I'm still doing around here." His words were spat with venom.

Was God using her to reach this man? She had to try. "Mary loves you."

"I know that," he snapped.

"Then why are you treating her so mean?"

"She deserves it."

Karen wanted to yell at him that her friend did not deserve the way he treated her. As she tried to figure out if she could outrun him, she asked, "What is it that's troubling you?" Yes, she could run faster, she figured. Especially since he'd been drinking.

He took another swig from his bottle. "I made a big mistake."

"By joining the Amish?"

"Yeah."

"Then why don't you talk to the bishop?"

"Talk to the Bishop, talk to the Bishop," he mimicked her. "You sound just like Mary."

"We'll that's what we do when we have a problem." She wanted to tell him that all problems could be sorted out because the bible had all the answers but she didn't want to sound like Aunt Agatha. She took a step away. "I hope everything works out for you."

"Why would you care?"

"Because Mary is my dear friend."

"I might as well jump in the river and drown. That would solve everyone's problems."

Even though she wanted to run, she stood still. If he was thinking of killing himself he'd think nothing of killing her. "I should be getting back now. I'm meeting someone at the *haus.*"

"Not so fast." He took a step toward her. "Why would you say you don't want someone to turn out like me?"

"I'm sorry, I didn't know you'd hear."

He yelled, "Just answer the question."

"I want my friend to be happy and you're making her miserable."

"Huh. It takes two to tango. She's making *me* miserable.

137

She's no clean potato. She's lazy. I work all day and come home and find out she's been out all day with her friends."

"I know she works for Samuel doing cleaning and she grows so many vegetables, so she's not lazy."

"The vegetables grow themselves. It takes no effort."

"She has to tend them, and she's not out all day with her friends because she only sees Beth and me on Sundays when there's no meeting."

"Then that's even worse. If she's not out with you … where is she?"

Now she'd made things worse for her friend. "Why do you find it necessary to drink every night?"

"Mary told you?"

"Maybe."

He threw the bottle down in a temper and she cringed at the glass shattering. He turned around and marched off. He was angry with Mary and now Karen didn't know what to do. "Wait." She hurried after him, but that made him go faster. "She didn't say that. Mary told me nothing." She ran fast and made a lunge at him. "Wait!" She grabbed his coat, unbalancing him, and then he fell hard. He was still. "Damian?" She leaned down and felt for a pulse. He was still breathing, she could hear it. She turned him over and then saw what she knew was blood on his forehead. He'd hit his head on one of the many large rocks that littered the shores of the river.

Through the trees, she saw the lights on in Mary's cottage. She had to get help. "Mary! Mary!" she kept screaming as she ran.

Mary opened the door. "Karen? What's wrong?"

"Damian's fallen. He hit his head on a rock and he's knocked out cold. Quick, we have to call an ambulance."

Mary grabbed a flashlight and the two of them ran to the phone in the barn.

After they called for the paramedics, Mary said, "I must go to him."

"They won't be long. We have to stay here so we can show them where he is."

"How did you both come to be by the river?"

Karen told her the whole story. A few minutes later, Karen breathed a sigh of relief as the sounds of sirens rang through the night air.

WITH LARGE FLASHLIGHTS, two paramedics followed Mary and Karen into the thickness of the trees. When they came to the spot Karen had left him, Damian wasn't there.

"Are you looking for me?" He came staggering toward them holding his head.

The two paramedics hurried toward him, as did Mary.

Karen pulled her back. "Let them treat him."

Mary trembled. "He'll blame me for this."

Karen didn't say anything. She hoped that the bump on the head might have knocked some sense into him. Mary lowered herself to the ground and sat sobbing.

"I'm so sorry, Karen. We had an argument and he walked off. It's what he always does. He never tells me about his problems or tells me why he's upset with me." Mary looked across at Damian. "I'll just see how he is."

"I'll come with you." Karen went with her, but stayed well back. She heard the paramedics telling Damian he should go to the hospital and get properly checked over.

"I'm okay," he insisted. He had a bandage around his head and was sitting on the ground propped against a tree trunk with his legs straight out and his shoulders slumped.

Mary said, "You should go, if they say so."

"What would you know? Do you have a medical degree?"

From where Karen stood, she could feel Mary's sadness. *"Nee*, but ..."

One of the paramedics turned to Mary and told her what signs to look for in case he got worse.

Karen was worried Mary would be left alone with him, but he certainly didn't look capable of physical violence tonight.

He looked up at Mary. "I'm sorry, Mary. I'll stop drinking."

"Do you mean it?".

He felt his bandage. "Yes, I mean it. This is not the kind of life for either of us, fighting all the time."

"We'll head off now," the same paramedic said to Mary.

"Thank you for all your help."

"We'll help you into the house." The paramedics helped him to his feet and after a couple of steps, he said, "I can walk myself."

Karen whispered to Mary. "I'll go now."

"Thanks for all your help." Mary gave Karen a quick hug before she walked inside with Damian.

KAREN FELT dreadful for being the cause of the accident in the first place. If she hadn't said unwise things to Mary's husband, he wouldn't have stormed off in a rage. If she hadn't grabbed his coat he might not have fallen. But, he had said sorry, said he'd quit drinking, so maybe this was all for the best. She hoped when Damian sobered up, he'd still be sorry. Karen walked back home, and then heated some leftovers for dinner.

WHEN THE MEATLOAF was heated through, she cut herself a portion and then took it into the living room and ate it on the couch with her feet propped up. When Jason came into her mind, she felt different. Instead of fear gnawing in her stomach, there was a sense of peace. It was as though something had clicked in her brain. Karen knew Jason would never let her down.

Now Karen was looking forward to seeing Jason again and hoped it wouldn't be too far away. She had said she'd give him an answer and now she knew what that answer would be. She hoped she hadn't ruined things by hesitating when he asked her to marry him.

JASON SAT down with his Uncle Peter and Aunt Barbara and their children. It was a happy home full of laughter. The young boys were at the age where they made up their own jokes and most of them weren't funny, which made the adults laugh all the more. More than anything, he wanted a family and a happy home just like this one. He knew he had to leave everything in God's hands. If Karen were the woman for him, her answer would be yes and if she turned him down he would go back home. His plan was to keep his distance until Karen approached him. He'd already made his intentions known and he didn't want to become a nuisance.

After dinner, there were games and then there was a bible reading before bedtime. The young boys asked questions, showing eager minds and hearts. Jason wondered what it was like to be a parent and guide young minds.

Jason felt at home in Pleasant Valley this trip and that probably had a lot to do with Karen. He could almost see and feel the happy life they would have together. He would make sure she never wore that worried face from the first time he had seen her. She was so pretty when she smiled.

CHAPTER 27

THE NEXT MORNING, Karen wondered if Mary and Damian were okay but she didn't want to intrude. She set off walking to Hannah and Bishop Elmer's house for her Saturday job. It was in the opposite direction from Mary and Damian's place, so she wouldn't be walking past it.

If she didn't see Jason today at Hannah's house, she decided to call him at Peter's house when she got home. She'd tell him she wanted to meet up with him. She'd tell him face-to-face yes, she'd marry him, and she wanted to tell him today before doubts set in.

The only hesitation she had was that he seemed a little lost and didn't know what he wanted to do with his life. She reasoned that since he was trained to do building work and had an injury, that was something that couldn't be helped. At least he was looking for new opportunities and the fact that he had traveled looking for those opportunities showed her he was making an effort and that was important.

She walked into Hannah's place and Rebecca was there sitting at the kitchen table. "I forgot it was Saturday. Is it Saturday?" Rebecca asked.

"It is, that's why I'm here. How is your *mudder?*"

"She's fine. She's just feeding the *boppli* upstairs."

"Did she leave any instructions for me?"

"*Nee*. I'll just run up and ask her what she wants you to do."

Karen looked around the spotless kitchen. "Did you do this?"

"*Jah*, it looks good, doesn't it? I just finished. If I'd known you were coming I would've left it." Rebecca giggled, and Karen laughed with her. "I'll just go see *Mamm.*"

"Okay."

Karen peeped into the laundry room and, as usual, there was a stack of dirty laundry. She started loading it into the washing machine and then the door behind her opened. It was the bishop.

"*Guder mariye,* Karen."

"Morning. How are you this fine day, Bishop Elmer?"

"*Wunderbaar.*"

She desperately wanted to tell him what had happened the night before, but Damian had apologized to Mary, so maybe things would work out between them after all. Then she saw people behind the bishop.

"Would you mind making us some coffee and tea, Karen?"

"Sure. For how many?"

"It's just me, Peter and Jason."

Her heart beat faster when he mentioned Jason. She wasn't ready to see him with other people around. "Sure."

Peter and Jason walked past her following the bishop. Each man greeted her and Karen reciprocated.

"Finish up what you were doing, and we'll be in the living room when you're ready, Karen."

"Okay." She nodded.

"Keep up the good work."

"I will." When she had closed the lid of the machine and

started it running, she filled the teakettle. Just as she finished, Rebecca came back into the room.

"I asked *Mamm* what she wants you to do and then forgot to come and tell you."

Karen rolled her eyes. Rebecca was always so forgetful. "Well, what did she say?"

"Washing the windows and the floors. And she wants you to take the rugs out to beat the dust out of them. She said I have to help you with that."

"Okay."

Without being told, Karen knew the routine when the family had visitors. She put tea in the teapot and filled it with hot water, placed mugs on the tray with the jug of milk and sugar, and added a carafe of hot coffee.

"You're leaving me with nothing to do," Rebecca said.

"I can't carry all this by myself. You'll have to help."

Rebecca took the coffee tray out to them and Karen carried the teapot.

KAREN HURRIED BACK to the kitchen when that was done. How was she supposed to clean the place with them sitting there? Normally the bishop took visitors into his office. She wondered what they were talking about as she returned to the laundry room.

"What are you going to do with your money, Karen?" Rebecca asked as she put things back into the cupboard. Karen began separating the whites and colors for the next loads as she answered, "I'm thinking of buying the house I'm living in now."

"Doesn't Samuel own it?"

"*Jah*, he does, but I've talked to him about buying it from him, and he said it might be a possibility."

"That's *wunderbaar*. I want to be just like you when I grow up."

"You're practically grown up now."

"I mean grown-up proper. And I guess I'll have to get my money through hard work."

"There's nothing wrong with hard work."

"You know what I'd really like to do, Karen? For a job, I mean?"

"What's that?"

"I want to be a midwife."

"That sounds like a good idea. There's so many women having babies all the time. Have you talked to Marilyn?"

"I have and she said after my next birthday, I could come to some appointments with her. And if the women agree, I can be present at their deliveries and start off as a birthing helper."

"That's a good profession, You have to be very dedicated and—"

"I know, I know. I got the whole speech from *Mamm*. I've got to be focused and I have to be ready to travel. I can't make any mistakes because lives are involved. I know all that."

"I'm glad you have thought it through."

"I have. And that's what I want to do. I just love babies."

"You've certainly been around them all your life."

Rebecca giggled. "I know. I have."

When Karen had done all she could do until the washing machine was finished, she swept the kitchen floor making her way to the doorway and closer to the men. They were engrossed in a conversation; she didn't like to deliberately eavesdrop, and even if she wanted to, she couldn't make out what they were saying.

AN HOUR LATER, the three men left in Peter's buggy. She was hoping she could have had a quiet word with Jason to tell him that she wanted to speak to him later that night. Now she would have to make a phone call later that day. Unless she just waited until Jason ... No, she couldn't wait. What if he changed his mind and left? She could not let that happen now that her heart had been opened to him.

CHAPTER 28

THAT NIGHT when Karen got home, she walked to the barn, picked up the phone's receiver and held it under her chin while she thumbed through her address book for Peter and Barbara's phone number. Almost as soon as she had dialed the last number, one of their boys answered the phone. "Hello?"

"Hello, would Jason be there please?"

"Sure. Hang on." Then she heard the boy yelling out for Jason.

Several seconds later she heard his voice. "Hello."

"Hi, Jason, it's Karen."

"Hi, Karen." Then there was silence.

"Can I see you sometime today, or tomorrow?" She held her breath.

"Today would be good. I can come there now."

"Could you?"

"*Jah,* sure. I'll see you soon."

"Okay." She placed the receiver back. This was it. The next conversation she had with Jason would shape their future. She walked out of the barn and had a look over at

Mary's house. It had been very quiet and she took that as a good sign.

When she got back inside her *haus,* she lit a lantern and took it out to the porch, placing it on the rustic wooden table. Then she raced inside to make sure she looked all right. When she was halfway through pulling on her favorite dress, she heard hoof beats. She finished dressing and straightened her *kapp* as she walked to the door.

She saw Jason jumping out of the buggy. He smiled and walked toward her as she leaned against the doorpost.

"What's all this about, Karen?" He raised his eyebrows and stopped five feet in front of her, paused a moment, and then slowly walked up the stone steps.

"I've been thinking about what you asked me the other day."

"And?" She knew by the way he asked that question that he was still interested. "Have you reached a decision?"

"My answer is yes."

A smile spread across his face. "You mean it? Really? You're not tricking me?"

She laughed and stepped forward, wanting to be held in his strong arms. "Why would I do that to you? It would be a pretty silly thing to do."

"I'm sorry." He chuckled. "I don't know if I should kiss you or jump up and down or what."

"A little kiss might be all right. Just one quick one wouldn't hurt."

He took her in his arms, bent his head down and kissed her on the lips. Her arms went around his neck; it seemed like a natural thing to do. When he stopped kissing her, she was disappointed. But she was certainly not disappointed with her decision which she now knew was the very right thing for both of them.

THAT EVENING, as they sat together in the lamplight on her porch, he told her everything about the bakery and the manager of the bakery who had cruelly ended their relationship to start one with another man. He also told her the lies Damian, Mary's husband, had told him about herself and Mary. Karen better understood then how upset he'd been that time when she wasn't there for his date. Even with these misunderstanding and through all the lies, God had been able to make a way.

Weeks later.

"HE WAS your last hope and I'm glad you took my advice."

Karen looked up at Aunt Agatha from the chair she sat in while Rebecca did her hair. Today was the day of Karen and Jason's wedding, and it was being held at the bishop's *haus.*

"Aunt Agatha, I'm sure she loves Jason," Rebecca said.

"I know. I didn't say she didn't. One must love one's husband."

"Aunt Agatha and I had a long conversation about marriage a while back."

"Oh." Rebecca continued brushing out Karen's long dark hair while Aunt Agatha moved to the window of Rebecca's upstairs bedroom. Rebecca still shared it with three of her younger brothers, but Karen had a surprise up her sleeve. She'd already given some of her inheritance money to the bishop to build on an extra room just for Rebecca.

"You'll remember today for the rest of your life, Karen."

"I know." She put her hand over her tummy. "I'm so excited I could barely eat breakfast."

Agatha looked back out the window. "And, he's just arrived."

"Jason?" Karen asked.

"*Jah.* He looks so handsome in his dark suit. Did you make it, Karen?"

"I helped her," Rebecca said. She placed the brush down and started braiding Karen's hair while Aunt Agatha, her nose pressed to the window, named everyone she saw arriving at the house.

The last weeks had been a whirlwind of wedding preparations. Karen had put a portion of her money into the house, leaving the rest in the bank, and Jason was going to put his into opening a bakery in town. He was in the middle of deciding on a location and Samuel was helping him. The two men seemed to be developing a good friendship. As for her two friends, Beth still hadn't gotten pregnant, but Mary's problems seemed like they had been resolved. Damian had meant his apology to Mary that night he'd hit his head. They'd had no arguments since, and he was keeping his word and getting help to overcome his drinking problem.

"Here's the rest of Jason's family," Aunt Agatha said. "How do you get along with them, Karen?"

"Just fine. I had dinner at Peter and Barbara's last night. That's where they're all staying."

"Hmm. They're leaving first thing in the morning."

"I know. Jason's *Dat* has to go back to work."

"You'll soon be married."

"I can't believe it. My life will soon change." Rather than visit relatives like other newly-married Amish couples, they planned to go back to their house and turn it into a real home. She wondered if she should've written to her birth mother to tell her the news. Something had stopped her from doing so. Deep down she felt certain nothing good would come of getting closer to that woman. A new door was opening in her life and she couldn't wait to go through it hand-in-hand with Jason. He was her family now.

HALF AN HOUR LATER, Jason and Karen stood before Bishop Elmer as he pronounced them married. Misty-eyed, Karen looked into Jason's loving blue eyes and her mind flashed back to the first time they'd seen each other in the bishop's laundry room.

Now they were married, and her every last fear was gone. God had found her a man who was perfect for her and there was only joy in her heart. She turned around to look at her friends, Mary and Beth. Right in the front row was Aunt Agatha with her face shining like a beacon. Karen smiled and turned back around, thinking now of her mother and father who'd loved her and raised her. They would've wanted to be there on her special day. She missed them badly and always would. To stop tears from falling, she reminded herself that the door of her old life was closed and a new door had opened. Her new husband took hold of her hand. She would walk through that door with Jason, always thankful for God's perfect plan.

JASON STARED down at his beautiful wife. Gone was the worried woman he'd seen at his uncle's house on that first day. In her place was a confident woman full of hope and love. He would be the best husband he could and strive to make sure she never frowned again. He hadn't come to Pleasant Valley looking for a wife, or even a girlfriend to replace the one who'd turned her back on him, but God had already had *His* plan in place.

≈

Thank you for reading
The Amish Woman and Her Last Hope.

～

The next books in the *Amish Women of Pleasant Valley*
series are:

Book 2 The Amish Woman and Her Secret Baby

Book 3 The Amish Widower's Promise

Book 4 The Amish Visitors

Book 5 The Amish Dreamer

Book 6 The Amish School Teacher

ABOUT THE AUTHOR

Samantha Price is a best selling author who knew she wanted to become a writer at the age of seven, while her grandmother read to her Peter Rabbit in the sun room. Though the adventures of Peter and his sisters Flopsy, Mopsy, and Cotton-tail started Samantha on her creative journey, it is now her love of Amish culture that inspires her to write. Her writing is clean and wholesome, with more than a dash of sweetness. Though she has penned over eighty Amish Romance and Amish Mystery books, Samantha is just as in love today with exploring the spiritual and emotional journeys of her characters as she was the day she first put pen to paper. Samantha lives in a quaint Victorian cottage with three rambunctious dogs.

www.samanthapriceauthor.com
samanthaprice333@gmail.com
www.facebook.com/SamanthaPriceAuthor
Follow Samantha Price on BookBub
Twitter @ AmishRomance